TABLE OF CONTENTS

CHAPTER 1: THE RETURN

CHAPTER 2: HAUNTED MEMORIES

CHAPTER 3: THE STRAIN OF SILENCE

CHAPTER 4: THE BOTTLE AND THE GUN

CHAPTER 5: REACHING OUT

CHAPTER 6: THE BURDEN OF GUILT

CHAPTER 7: STEPS TOWARD HEALING

CHAPTER 8: A NEW BATTLE

CHAPTER 9: CONFRONTING THE PAST

CHAPTER 10: THE LONG ROAD AHEAD

THE LONG ROAD HOME: A SOLDIER'S JOURNEY TO PEACE

CHAPTER 1: THE RETURN

Jack Reynolds stepped off the plane into the warm embrace of a summer afternoon, but the sun's rays barely reached him. The sounds of the bustling airport, the distant hum of engines, and the chatter of travelers all seemed muffled, as if he were hearing them through a thick fog. He scanned the crowd, searching for a familiar face among the sea of strangers. Then he saw them—Emma and Lily—waiting just beyond the security checkpoint.

Emma waved excitedly, her smile radiant as she held their daughter in her arms. Lily, now six years old, had grown so much since Jack had last seen her. She waved a small American flag, her eyes wide with excitement as she spotted her father. Jack forced a smile and quickened his pace, though his legs felt like lead.

"Welcome home, Jack!" Emma cried as she threw her arms around him. Lily wriggled out of her mother's grasp and hugged Jack's leg, holding on tightly. Jack embraced them both, burying his face in Emma's hair and inhaling the scent of home—lavender and vanilla.

"I missed you so much," Emma whispered, her voice trembling with emotion.

"I missed you too," Jack replied, his voice sounding hollow to his own ears. He kissed Emma's forehead, then knelt to Lily's level, pulling her into a tight hug. Lily giggled, wrapping her arms around his neck.

"Daddy, you're finally home!" she exclaimed, her voice bright and full of joy. "Did you bring me a present?"

Jack forced another smile, reaching into his bag to produce a small, hand-carved wooden doll he had bought at a market overseas. Lily's eyes lit up as she took the doll, examining it with fascination.

"It's beautiful, Daddy! Thank you!" She gave him another hug before running ahead toward the car, the doll clutched tightly in her hand.

Emma slipped her hand into Jack's as they walked to the parking lot. "It's so good to have you back," she said softly, squeezing his hand. "You're home now."

Home. The word hung in the air between them, heavy with unspoken meaning. Jack had dreamed of this moment countless times during his deployment—of the day he would finally return to the life he had left behind. But now that he was here, standing beside his wife and daughter, the life he had once known felt like a distant memory.

As they drove home, Jack stared out the window, watching the familiar landscape pass by. The small suburban town he had grown up in looked unchanged, with its tree-lined streets, well-kept lawns, and white picket fences. But to Jack, everything seemed different, as if he were seeing it all for the first time through a distorted lens.

Emma kept the conversation light, asking Jack about his flight, their plans for the weekend, and how excited Lily was to show him the picture she had drawn for him at school. Jack answered her questions, but his responses were short, his mind elsewhere.

When they pulled into the driveway of their modest two-story home, Jack felt a strange sense of detachment, as if he were watching the scene unfold from outside his own body. The house was exactly as he remembered it—white siding, blue shutters, a small garden in the front yard that Emma had tended to with care. Yet, it felt unfamiliar, like a place he no longer belonged.

"Come on, Daddy!" Lily called as she jumped out of the car and ran toward the front door. "I want to show you my room!"

Jack followed her inside, trying to shake the feeling of unease that had settled over him. He stepped into the living room, where the smell of fresh-baked cookies greeted him. The walls were adorned with family photos—snapshots of happier times. His and Emma's wedding day, Lily's first steps, a family vacation at the beach. But those moments felt like they belonged to someone else, a different version of Jack who no longer existed.

"Daddy, look!" Lily called from the top of the stairs. "I made you a drawing!"

Jack climbed the stairs slowly, his legs heavy with fatigue. When he reached Lily's room, she proudly held up a crayon drawing of the three of them standing in front of their house, smiling under a bright yellow sun.

"Do you like it?" Lily asked, her eyes wide with anticipation.

Jack knelt beside her and studied the drawing. It was a simple, innocent depiction of their family—a family that Jack no longer felt a part of. He swallowed hard, forcing down the lump in his throat.

"It's beautiful, sweetheart," he said, his voice strained. He pulled her into a hug, holding her tightly as if trying to anchor himself to the present.

Lily beamed, then ran off to play with her new doll, leaving Jack alone in the room. He stood up and looked around, taking in the familiar surroundings. The pink walls, the stuffed animals on the bed, the bookshelf filled with children's stories—all of it should have brought him comfort, but instead, it only deepened his sense of alienation.

He heard Emma's footsteps behind him and turned to see her standing in the doorway, concern etched on her face.

"Are you okay?" she asked, her voice gentle.

Jack nodded, though he knew he wasn't convincing her. "Yeah, I'm just tired. It's been a long trip."

Emma stepped closer, placing a hand on his arm. "I know it's going to take some time to adjust. But we're here for you, Jack. Whatever you need, we'll get through this together."

Jack forced a smile and kissed her on

the forehead. "I know," he said, though he wasn't sure he believed it. He wanted to believe it, wanted to believe that he could find his way back to the life he had before the war. But deep down, he knew that the man who had left for deployment wasn't the same man who had come back.

As the day wore on, Jack went through the motions of being home. He helped Emma set the table for dinner, listened to Lily chatter about school, and tried to engage in conversation. But all the while, he felt a growing distance between himself and his family, as if an invisible barrier separated him from the life he once knew.

That night, after Lily had gone to bed, Jack sat alone on the back porch, staring out at the darkened yard. The crickets chirped in the distance, and the cool night air brushed against his skin. But the peacefulness of the scene only served to amplify the turmoil inside him.

He closed his eyes, trying to will away the memories that threatened to surface. The explosions, the gunfire, the cries for help—it was all still so vivid, so real. He could feel the weight of the rifle in his hands, smell the acrid scent of burning debris, hear the anguished voices of the people he couldn't save.

Jack opened his eyes and took a deep breath, trying to steady himself. He had made it home. He was safe now. But the war hadn't stayed behind—it had followed him, embedding itself in his mind like a virus that he couldn't shake.

The front door creaked open, and Jack turned to see Emma stepping out onto the porch. She sat down beside him, slipping her hand into his.

"You've been quiet," she said softly. "Do you want to talk about it?"

Jack shook his head, unable to find the words. How could he explain what he was feeling when he didn't fully understand it himself? How could he share the weight of the things he had seen and done when he couldn't even bear it alone?

Emma didn't press him. She simply sat with him in silence, her hand warm in his. For a moment, Jack allowed himself to lean into her presence, to take comfort in the fact that she was here, that she hadn't given up on him.

But the comfort was fleeting, quickly replaced by the gnawing sense of guilt that had become his constant companion. He had survived when so many others hadn't. He had come home when others had been left behind. And now, here he was, surrounded by the people he loved, yet feeling more alone than ever.

Jack stared out into the darkness, the weight of his thoughts pressing down on him. The road ahead seemed long and uncertain, filled with obstacles he wasn't sure he could overcome. But as he sat there, with Emma by his side, he knew one thing for certain: the war was far from over. The battle to find his way back home, to truly come home, had only just begun.

CHAPTER 2: HAUNTED MEMORIES

Jack jolted awake, his heart pounding, the remnants of his nightmare clinging to him like a heavy fog. He lay still in the darkness, his breath ragged, trying to steady himself. The familiar surroundings of his bedroom—the soft glow of the alarm clock, the faint hum of the ceiling fan—did little to calm him. The terror that had gripped him in sleep still lingered, a cold dread seeping into his bones.

He sat up slowly, careful not to wake Emma, who was sleeping soundly beside him. Her even breathing was a stark contrast to the chaos that raged inside him. Jack swung his legs over the side of the bed and pressed his feet into the cool floor, grounding himself in the present. But no matter how hard he tried, the memories surged forward, unbidden.

In his mind, he was back in the desert, the scorching heat pressing down on him, the air thick with the smell of burning oil and dust. The memory came to him in flashes—the crack of gunfire, the shouts of his men, the distant roar of an explosion. And then, the faces of the civilians—terrified, desperate—caught in the crossfire.

Jack squeezed his eyes shut, trying to block out the images, but they only became more vivid. He could see the aftermath of the raid, the bodies strewn across the ground, the blood soaking into the dirt. He could hear the cries of the wounded, the pleas for help that he couldn't answer. And above it all, the sickening realization that he had been the one to give the order, the one who had condemned them to die.

His hands clenched into fists, the knuckles white with strain. He felt like he was suffocating, the weight of his guilt pressing down on him, crushing him. The faces of the dead haunted him, their lifeless eyes accusing him in the darkness.

Jack stood abruptly, needing to escape the confines of the bedroom, the suffocating closeness of the walls. He slipped out of the room and into the hallway, his steps careful and quiet. The house was still, the only sound the creak of the floorboards beneath his feet. He made his way downstairs, where the living room lay shrouded in shadow.

He moved to the window and looked out into the night. The moon cast a pale light over the yard, the trees swaying gently in the breeze. It was peaceful, a stark contrast to the storm that raged within him. But no matter how hard he tried, Jack couldn't reconcile the tranquility of his surroundings with the violence that consumed his mind.

The memories came back to him in waves—his time in the war, the missions that had gone wrong, the lives that had been lost. He could still hear the voices of his comrades, see the fear in their eyes as they faced death together. And always, at the center of it all, was that one moment, that one decision that had changed everything.

Jack's thoughts drifted back to that day, the day that had come to define his nightmares. His unit had been sent to clear out a suspected insurgent stronghold in a small village. The intelligence had been solid, or so they thought. But when they arrived, it quickly became clear that something was wrong.

They had moved in fast, following the protocol drilled into them during training. But as they breached the compound, it became clear that the intel had been flawed. There were no insurgents, no enemy fighters—only civilians. Women, children, and old men, all caught in the chaos of war.

Jack's heart had raced as he realized the mistake, but by then it was too late. The gunfire had erupted, and in the confusion, lives were lost—innocent lives. He had tried to call off the attack, to order his men to hold their fire, but the damage had been done. The village was left in ruins, the bodies of the dead a testament to their error.

The weight of that day had never left him. It clung to him like a shadow, following him even now, back home, thousands of miles away from the battlefield. The guilt was relentless, gnawing at him, tearing at the edges of his sanity.

Jack leaned his forehead against the cool glass of the window, his breath fogging the pane. He had survived the war, but at what cost? He had left a piece of himself behind in that village, a piece he would never get back.

A sound behind him made Jack turn. Emma stood at the base of the stairs, her expression a mix of concern and exhaustion. She was wearing the robe he had given her before he left, the one she had promised to wear every night until he returned. It hung loosely around her, and Jack could see the lines of worry etched into her face, lines he knew he had put there.

"Jack," she said softly, her voice heavy with sleep, "are you okay?"

He opened his mouth to respond, but the words wouldn't come. How could he explain what he was feeling? How could he make her understand the darkness that had taken root inside him?

Emma crossed the room to stand beside him, placing a gentle hand on his arm. "You've been having nightmares again, haven't you?"

Jack nodded, unable to meet her gaze. The nightmares were nothing new—they had started during his first deployment, growing more vivid and terrifying with each passing year. But since he had returned home, they had taken on a new intensity, as if the memories had been waiting for the right moment to resurface.

"Do you want to talk about it?" she asked, her voice full of concern.

Jack shook his head. He didn't want to burden her with the horrors that plagued him, didn't want to drag her down into the darkness that consumed him. "I'm fine," he lied, forcing a smile that didn't reach his eyes. "I just couldn't sleep."

Emma studied him for a moment, as if trying to see past the facade he had put up. She knew him too well to be fooled, but she didn't push. Instead, she wrapped her arms around him, pulling him into a tight embrace.

"You don't have to go through this alone," she whispered, her voice thick with emotion. "I'm here for you, Jack. Whatever you need, I'm here."

Jack closed his eyes, resting his chin on the top of her head. He wanted to believe her, wanted to let her in, but he couldn't. The weight of his guilt was too heavy, the memories too painful to share. He had been a soldier for so long, had learned to compartmentalize, to keep his emotions in check. It was all he knew.

But now, back in the safety of his home, those walls were crumbling. The

nightmares were only the beginning—
each day, the memories grew stronger,
more intrusive, seeping into his waking
hours. He saw the faces of the dead in
every corner of the house, heard their
cries in the silence of the night. They
haunted him, a constant reminder of
the man he had become.

Jack pulled away from Emma, offering
her another forced smile. "I'm fine," he
repeated, though the words felt hollow
in his mouth. "Go back to bed. I'll be up
in a minute."

Emma hesitated, searching his eyes for
something, but whatever she saw there
must have convinced her to let it go.
She nodded, giving his hand a final
squeeze before heading back upstairs.

Jack watched her go, feeling a pang of
guilt for pushing her away. She
deserved better—better than a husband
who was haunted by the past, better

than a man who couldn't leave the war behind. But no matter how hard he tried, he couldn't shake the darkness that had taken hold of him.

As the house fell silent once more, Jack sank into the armchair by the window, his head in his hands. The nightmares would return, he knew they would, but for now, he would sit here and wait for the dawn, the memories pressing down on him like a heavy weight.

He had survived the war, but the battle was far from over. The ghosts of his past were relentless, and no matter how far he ran, they always caught up with him. Jack knew that he couldn't keep this up forever—something had to give. But for now, he would endure, because that's what he had been trained to do.

And so, as the first light of dawn crept over the horizon, Jack sat alone with his thoughts, the memories of the dead his only company.

CHAPTER 3: THE STRAIN OF SILENCE

Days turned into weeks, and Jack's sense of alienation only deepened. He moved through life as if in a daze, doing his best to fulfill the roles expected of him—a husband, a father, a neighbor. But no matter how hard he tried, he couldn't shake the feeling that he was living someone else's life. The distance between him and Emma grew wider, an unspoken chasm that neither of them knew how to cross.

It started with the little things. Jack found himself retreating into silence more often, answering Emma's questions with monosyllables, if he responded at all. He would sit at the dinner table, pushing food around his plate, his mind far from the conversations that swirled around him. Lily's laughter, once a sound that filled him with joy, now seemed distant, as if it were happening in another room. Even the home he had longed to return to felt like a place where he didn't belong.

Emma tried to reach him. She would sit beside him on the couch, leaning into him as they watched television, but Jack would stiffen, his body tense. She would ask him to go for walks with her, to spend time in the garden where they used to laugh and talk for hours, but Jack would always find an excuse to stay inside. Each time she tried to bridge the gap between them, Jack pulled further away, retreating into a shell that felt increasingly impenetrable.

One evening, after another silent dinner, Emma finally confronted him. She had been patient, understanding in a way that Jack felt he didn't deserve. But even she had her limits.

"Jack, we need to talk," she said, her voice firm but gentle. She stood in the doorway of the living room, where Jack sat staring blankly at the television. The show that played across the screen held no interest for him; he hadn't even registered what it was.

Jack sighed inwardly, dreading this conversation but knowing it was inevitable. He muted the television and turned to face her; his expression guarded.

"What's going on with you?" Emma asked, stepping closer. "You've been so distant since you got home. I feel like I'm losing you."

Jack looked down at his hands, his knuckles white from clenching them too tightly. "I'm fine, Emma. I'm just...tired. It's been a lot to adjust to, that's all."

Emma shook her head, frustration flashing in her eyes. "No, it's more than that, Jack. You're shutting me out, and I don't know why. I know things were hard over there, but you're home now. We're supposed to be a team, remember?"

Jack felt a pang of guilt, but it was quickly swallowed by the numbness that had settled over him since his return. "I don't want to burden you with all that," he said, his voice flat. "It's not something you need to deal with."

Emma's face softened, and she reached out to take his hand. "You're my husband, Jack. Whatever you're going through, we're supposed to go through it together. You don't have to carry this alone."

Jack pulled his hand away, standing up abruptly. "You wouldn't understand, Emma. You weren't there. You didn't see the things I saw."

Emma flinched at his harsh tone but didn't back down. "Then help me understand," she pleaded. "Talk to me, Jack. Let me in."

But Jack couldn't. The memories were too raw, too painful to share. The things he had done, the lives that had been lost because of his decisions—it was too much. He couldn't bring that darkness into their home, into their lives. It was his burden to bear, and he would bear it alone.

"I can't," he said, his voice breaking. "I just...can't."

Emma's eyes filled with tears, and for a moment, Jack thought she would push him further, demand that he opens up. But instead, she stepped back, her expression one of defeat.

"I'm here when you're ready," she said quietly, turning away and walking back toward the kitchen.

Jack stood alone in the living room, the sound of Emma's footsteps fading down the hall. He felt a knot of anger and frustration tightening in his chest, but he didn't know who it was directed at— himself, for failing to be the husband and father his family needed, or Emma, for asking him to open wounds that hadn't even begun to heal.

He ran a hand through his hair, trying to dispel the tension that had built up in his body. But the anger remained, simmering just beneath the surface. He wanted to smash something, to lash out at the world for putting him in this position. But he knew that would solve nothing. It would only push Emma and Lily further away.

Jack left the living room and headed

upstairs to their bedroom, hoping the solitude might offer some relief. He closed the door behind him and leaned against it, his eyes shut tight as he tried to block out the images that flooded his mind. But they came anyway, unbidden and relentless.

He saw the faces of the civilians from the village again—women and children, their eyes wide with fear as gunfire tore through the air. He heard the shouts of his men, the confusion, the panic, and the sickening realization that they had made a terrible mistake. He saw the bodies crumpling to the ground, the blood pooling around them, and the look of horror on the face of a young boy as he stared up at Jack, his life slipping away.

Jack pressed the heels of his hands against his eyes, as if he could somehow push the memories out of his mind. But they were etched there, a permanent scar that refused to heal.

He moved to the bed and sat down heavily, his head in his hands. How could he explain any of this to Emma? How could he make her understand that the man she had married no longer existed? That the war had taken him and replaced him with someone else—someone who couldn't leave the battlefield behind?

He didn't know how long he sat there, lost in his thoughts, before Emma came into the room. She didn't say anything, just quietly changed into her pajamas and slipped into bed. Jack could feel the tension in the air between them, the unspoken words that hung there like a dark cloud. He lay down beside her, keeping his distance, the silence between them heavy and oppressive.

As the minutes ticked by, the weight of the silence became unbearable. Jack wanted to reach out, to bridge the gap that had formed between them, but he couldn't find the words. What could he possibly say that would make any of this better? How could he explain the darkness that had taken hold of him without dragging Emma down with him?

He turned onto his side, his back to her, and closed his eyes. But sleep didn't come. Instead, the memories played out in his mind like a film reel, over and over, refusing to let him rest.

The next morning, the strain was evident in every interaction. Emma moved through the house with a forced cheerfulness, but Jack could see the hurt in her eyes, the way she avoided looking at him directly. Lily, always perceptive, picked up on the tension and became quieter, her usual exuberance dimmed by the unease that now permeated their home.

Jack hated himself for what he was doing to them, for bringing the war home with him and letting it poison the life they had built. But no matter how hard he tried; he couldn't break free from the grip it had on him. The guilt, the nightmares, the memories—they were all consuming, and they were tearing him apart from the inside out.

Days turned into weeks, and the distance between Jack and Emma grew more pronounced. He found himself spending more time away from home, avoiding the places and people that reminded him of the life he could no longer fully participate in. He started taking long drives with no destination, just driving for hours, trying to escape the thoughts that chased him wherever he went.

Emma continued to reach out to him, her patience admirable but increasingly strained. She would leave notes in his lunchbox, little reminders that she loved him and was there for him, but Jack found it harder and harder to respond. The guilt of his silence weighed on him, but the fear of confronting his past was even greater.

He knew that something had to give, that he couldn't continue living in this limbo, caught between the life he had known and the memories he couldn't escape. But he didn't know how to move forward, how to take that first step toward healing without losing himself in the process.

One night, after another dinner marked by awkward silences and forced smiles, Emma cornered him in the kitchen. She had been patient, more patient than Jack deserved, but he could see the frustration and hurt etched in her features.

"Jack, I don't know how much longer I can do this," she said, her voice trembling. "I'm trying to be here for you, but you keep pushing me away. I feel like I'm losing you, and I don't know what to do."

Jack looked down at the floor, unable to meet her gaze. "I'm sorry, Emma. I'm just... I'm not ready to talk about it."

Emma's eyes filled with tears, but she blinked them back, refusing to let them fall. "You don't have to do this alone," she said, her voice barely above a whisper. "We're a family, Jack. We're supposed to face things together."

Jack swallowed hard; his throat tight. He knew she was right, knew that he was hurting her with his silence. But the thought of opening up, of letting her see the darkness that had taken hold of him, was terrifying. He felt like he was teetering on the edge of a precipice, and one wrong step would send him plummeting into the abyss.

"I don't want to hurt you," Jack finally said, his voice strained. "I've seen things, done things... I'm not the same man I was when I left. I don't know how to be that person again."

Emma took a step closer, her expression softening as she reached out to touch his arm. "I know you've been through hell, Jack. But shutting me out isn't the answer. I can't help you if you won't let me in."

Jack looked at her, really looked at her, for the first time in what felt like weeks. He could see the love and concern in her eyes, the pain she was trying so hard to hide. She was right; they were supposed to face things together. But the thought of laying his soul bare, of sharing the burden of his guilt and trauma, was too overwhelming.

"I'm scared, Emma," he admitted, his voice barely a whisper. It was the first time he had spoken those words out loud, the first time he had acknowledged the fear that had been gnawing at him since the day he came home.

Emma's eyes softened, and she stepped closer, wrapping her arms around him. Jack stiffened at first, but then, slowly, he relaxed into her embrace, letting himself be held.

"You don't have to do this alone," Emma whispered into his ear, her voice thick with emotion. "I'm here. I'll always be here. But you must let me in, Jack. We can't get through this if you keep shutting me out."

Jack closed his eyes, fighting back the tears that threatened to spill. He wanted so badly to let her in, to share the weight of his pain, but the fear of what she might think, of how she might see him differently, held him back.

"I don't know how," he finally said, his voice cracking with the weight of his confession.

Emma pulled back slightly, just enough to look him in the eyes. "One step at a time," she said softly. "We'll figure it out together. But you must take that first step, Jack. You must let me help you."

Jack stared at her, the woman he had promised to love and cherish, the woman who had stood by him through the worst of it. She was right—he had to take that first step, no matter how terrifying it was.

"I'll try," he said, his voice trembling. It was all he could offer in that moment, but it was the truth.

Emma smiled, a small, sad smile, but a smile, nonetheless. "That's all I ask," she said, her voice gentle. "Just try."

For the first time in weeks, Jack felt a small flicker of hope. It wasn't much, but it was something. He knew he wasn't anywhere close to being okay, but maybe, just maybe, he could find a way to start healing.

They stood there in the kitchen, holding each other, the silence between them no longer oppressive but comforting. Jack still didn't know how he was going to move forward, but for the first time, he didn't feel completely alone.

Over the next few days, Jack made a conscious effort to be more present, to engage with Emma and Lily, even if it was just in small ways. He helped Lily with her homework, listened as she talked about her day at school, and even managed to smile at her jokes. He tried to talk to Emma more, to let her in, even though it was still difficult.

But despite his efforts, the nightmares continued. Every night, the memories would come back, vivid and relentless, dragging him back to the desert, to the faces of the civilians he had failed to protect. And every morning, he would wake up exhausted, the weight of his guilt pressing down on him like a physical force.

One particularly bad night, Jack woke up drenched in sweat, his heart racing. He could still hear the screams, the sound of gunfire echoing in his ears. He sat up in bed, trying to steady his breathing, but the panic wouldn't subside.

Emma stirred beside him, waking up as she felt him move. She turned to him, her eyes still heavy with sleep, but filled with concern.

"Jack?" she asked softly, reaching out to touch his arm. "Another nightmare?"

Jack nodded, unable to speak. He felt like he was suffocating, the memories closing in on him, trapping him.

Emma sat up beside him, her hand rubbing soothing circles on his back. "It's okay," she whispered. "You're safe. You're home."

But Jack didn't feel safe. He felt like he was still in the middle of the battle, the chaos and violence all around him. He wanted to scream, to cry, to do something to release the pressure building inside him, but he couldn't. He was trapped in his own mind, a prisoner of his memories.

"I can't... I can't do this," he finally choked out, his voice breaking. "It's too much."

Emma didn't say anything, just continued to rub his back, her touch grounding him, reminding him that he wasn't alone.

"You don't have to do it alone," she said softly after a while. "We'll get through this together, Jack. I promise."

Jack wanted to believe her, wanted to trust that they could get through this, but the fear and guilt still held him in their grip.

The next morning, after a long, sleepless night, Emma suggested that Jack consider talking to someone— someone who understood what he was going through. Jack resisted at first, the idea of therapy or a support group feeling foreign and uncomfortable. But as the days passed and the nightmares persisted, he began to realize that he couldn't do this alone. He needed help, and if he wanted to keep his family together, he had to find a way to heal.

Reluctantly, Jack agreed to look into a veterans' support group. It wasn't an easy decision—every instinct told him to keep his pain buried, to deal with it on his own. But he knew that if he didn't do something, he would lose everything—his family, his sanity, his life.

As Jack sat in front of the computer that night, searching for local veterans' groups, Emma came up behind him, resting a hand on his shoulder.

"You're doing the right thing," she said softly. "It's a big step, Jack."

He nodded, still feeling uncertain but knowing he had to try. "I hope so," he said quietly. "I just... I don't know if I can do this."

Emma squeezed his shoulder gently. "You can. And I'll be right here with you, every step of the way."

Jack closed his eyes, taking a deep breath. It was a small step, but it was a step toward healing. He didn't know what the future held, didn't know if he would ever be able to shake the nightmares, the guilt, the memories. But for the first time, he wasn't facing it alone. He had Emma by his side, and maybe, just maybe, that would be enough to help him find his way back to the man he used to be.

CHAPTER 4: THE BOTTLE AND THE GUN

Jack sat alone in the darkened living room, a half-empty bottle of whiskey on the coffee table in front of him. The amber liquid glowed faintly in the dim light, a bitter comfort in his hand as he took another swig. The burn of the alcohol down his throat was the only thing that seemed real, the only thing that cut through the fog of his thoughts.

The house was silent, save for the faint ticking of the clock on the wall. Emma and Lily had gone to bed hours ago, leaving Jack to wrestle with his demons in solitude. He knew he was falling apart—each day, the nightmares grew worse, the memories more vivid, the guilt more consuming. The support group had helped a little, but it was like trying to hold back a flood with a dam made of paper.

Jack stared at the bottle in his hand, his vision blurring as the alcohol took its toll. He knew he was drinking too much, using the whiskey to dull the pain he couldn't escape. But he didn't care. The numbness was better than the constant ache, better than the relentless barrage of memories that tore at him day and night.

But even the whiskey couldn't keep the thoughts at bay tonight. They crept in around the edges of his consciousness, slithering through the cracks in his armor, no matter how much he drank. The images of the civilians he had killed, the sound of their dying breaths, the feel of his finger on the trigger—they were all there, waiting for him in the darkness.

Jack took another drink, but it wasn't enough. The memories kept coming, the faces of the dead haunting him, accusing him, refusing to let him rest. He could see the young boy again, the one who had looked up at him with wide, terrified eyes as he lay bleeding out in the dirt. Jack had tried to save him, but it was too late. The boy had died in his arms, his small body growing limp as the life drained out of him.

The bottle slipped from Jack's hand, clattering to the floor, the whiskey spilling out across the carpet. He didn't bother to pick it up. He just stared at it, the liquid seeping into the fibers, spreading like the blood that had pooled around the boy's body.

Jack's breath hitched in his throat, a sob rising unbidden from his chest. He had kept it all inside for so long, burying the pain, the guilt, the fear deep down where no one could see it. But now it was all coming to the surface, overwhelming him, crushing him under its weight.

He couldn't do this anymore. The thought hit him like a sledgehammer, cold and final. He couldn't keep pretending that everything was okay, that he could somehow find his way back to the man he used to be. That man was gone, and all that was left was a broken shell, a hollowed-out husk consumed by guilt and shame.

The realization settled over him, bringing with it a terrible sense of calm. For the first time in months, the noise in his head quieted, the chaos giving way to a single, clear thought: it would be better if he wasn't here anymore.

Jack rose from the couch on unsteady legs, his heart pounding in his chest as he made his way to the bedroom. The door creaked softly as he pushed it open, the sound almost deafening in the stillness of the house. He stood in the doorway, watching Emma and Lily as they slept, their faces peaceful, oblivious to the storm that raged inside him.

He wanted to remember them like this—safe, untouched by the darkness that had consumed him. He wanted to believe that they would be better off without him, that his absence would be less painful than the presence of the man he had become. He had failed them, failed to be the husband and father they deserved. Leaving would be the last good thing he could do for them.

Jack's hand trembled as he reached for the gun in the nightstand drawer. It was the same gun he had carried with him during his deployments, a familiar weight in his palm. It had saved his life more times than he could count, and now, it would end it.

He walked back to the living room, the gun clutched tightly in his hand. The whiskey still soaked into the carpet, the bottle lying on its side, forgotten. Jack sat down on the floor, leaning back against the couch, the gun resting in his lap. The cold metal felt solid, grounding him in the moment as he tried to gather his thoughts.

He didn't want to leave a note. What could he possibly say? Sorry wasn't enough. It wouldn't make up for the years of pain he was about to inflict on Emma and Lily. It wouldn't erase the memories that would haunt them, the questions they would never have answers to. But at least they wouldn't have to watch him fall apart, wouldn't have to bear witness to his slow, inevitable unraveling.

Jack lifted the gun, the barrel cold against his temple. His finger hovered over the trigger, his breath coming in shallow, ragged gasps. He squeezed his eyes shut, trying to push away the fear, the doubt that gnawed at the edges of his resolve. He couldn't back out now, couldn't let the pain drag on any longer.

In the silence, he heard a small voice, quiet but unmistakable. "Daddy?"

Jack's eyes flew open, his heart leaping into his throat as he turned to see Lily standing in the doorway, her stuffed bear clutched tightly in her arms. She looked so small, so vulnerable in the dim light, her wide eyes filled with confusion.

"Daddy, what are you doing?" she asked, her voice trembling. She took a step closer, her gaze flicking to the gun in his hand, and then back to his face.

Jack froze, the gun still pressed against his temple, his finger on the trigger.

Time seemed to stop, the world narrowing to the space between him and his daughter. He couldn't move, couldn't breathe, as he stared into her eyes, the weight of his actions crashing down on him like a tidal wave.

Lily took another step closer, her lower lip trembling as she looked up at him. "Daddy why are you crying?"

Jack hadn't realized he was crying until she said it. The tears streamed down his face, hot and unrelenting, and his chest heaved with sobs he couldn't hold back. He wanted to reach out to her, to pull her into his arms and tell her that everything was okay, but he couldn't. He couldn't lie to her, not anymore.

"Lily," he choked out, his voice breaking. "I'm so sorry."

Lily dropped her bear and rushed to him, throwing her arms around his neck, her small body shaking with fear. "Daddy don't be sad," she whispered, her voice thick with tears. "Please don't be sad."

Jack's resolve shattered. The gun slipped from his hand, falling to the floor with a dull thud as he wrapped his arms around his daughter, holding her as tightly as he could. The sobs tore through him, uncontrollable, as he buried his face in her hair, the scent of her shampoo filling his senses.

"I'm so sorry, baby," he sobbed, his voice raw. "I'm so sorry."

Lily held him, her small hands clutching at his shirt, her tears soaking into his collar. "It's okay, Daddy," she whispered, her voice soft but steady. "It's okay."

Jack didn't know how long they sat there, wrapped in each other's arms, the weight of what he had almost done pressing down on him like a physical force. He had been seconds away from leaving her, from leaving them both, and the thought made him sick to his core.

When he finally pulled back, Lily looked up at him with wide, tear-filled eyes. "Can we go back to bed now, Daddy?" she asked, her voice small and tired.

Jack nodded, his throat too tight to speak. He picked her up, cradling her against his chest as he carried her back to her room. He laid her down gently in her bed, pulling the covers up to her chin, and sat beside her until her breathing evened out, the rise and fall of her chest slow and steady.

As he watched her sleep, the enormity of what had just happened hit him with full force. He had almost left his daughter to grow up without a father, almost abandoned his wife to deal with the fallout of his death. He had been so consumed by his own pain that he hadn't seen the pain he was about to inflict on the people he loved most in the world.

Jack felt a wave of nausea roll through him, and he stumbled to the bathroom, barely making it to the toilet before he threw up, his body rejecting the whiskey and the despair that had nearly destroyed him. He collapsed onto the cold tile floor, his body wracked with tremors as the realization of what he had almost done settled over him.

When he finally dragged himself back to his feet, he caught a glimpse of himself in the bathroom mirror. His reflection stared back at him, hollow-eyed and pale, a stranger in his own skin. The man who had looked back at him just hours earlier was gone, replaced by someone who had come terrifyingly close to losing everything.

Jack knew he couldn't go on like this. He had reached the edge, and there was no going back. He needed help, real help, not just the support group or the whiskey. He needed to face the demons that had driven him to this point, or he wouldn't survive.

He washed his face, splashing cold water over his face, trying to cleanse the remnants of the night's ordeal. The cold water stung his skin, but it was nothing compared to the pain that had gripped him just moments ago. Jack stared at his reflection, droplets of water trickling down his face, mingling with the tears that hadn't yet dried.

His reflection was a haunting reminder of how far he had fallen. The man who had once stood tall, proud of his service, was gone. In his place was someone broken, someone who had almost given up, who had come terrifyingly close to abandoning everything and everyone who mattered to him. The realization was suffocating, but it was also grounding—forcing him to confront the stark truth that he could not continue down this path.

He wiped his face with a towel, then left the bathroom, walking back into the living room where the gun still lay on the floor, a cold, metallic reminder of what he had nearly done. Jack stood over it for a moment, his chest tightening with a mix of shame and fear. He knelt slowly, picking it up with trembling hands. The weight of it felt different now—no longer an escape, but a symbol of the darkness he had allowed to take hold of him.

Jack knew he had to get rid of it. Keeping the gun in the house was a risk he couldn't afford to take. He walked back to the bedroom, where Emma still slept peacefully, unaware of the turmoil that had unfolded just a few rooms away. Jack quietly opened the drawer of the nightstand and placed the gun inside, pushing it far back, out of sight, as if doing so could somehow push the night's events out of his mind. But he knew better. This was a wound that would take time to heal, and the scars would never fully fade.

As he stood over Emma, watching her sleep, Jack felt a deep, aching love for her—a love that was tangled up in guilt and fear. He had almost left her to face life alone, to raise their daughter without him, to bear the weight of his decision. The thought made his heart ache, and he vowed silently, desperately, that he would never let himself get to that point again.

But the vow wasn't enough. He knew that now. Words alone wouldn't save him. He needed action—needed to take the first, terrifying step toward getting the help he so desperately needed.

Jack turned away from the bed and walked back to the living room, the house eerily quiet in the aftermath of his breakdown. He sat down on the couch, the faint smell of spilled whiskey lingering in the air. The silence was oppressive, but it was better than the storm that had raged inside him just hours before.

The stillness gave him time to think, to process what had happened and what he needed to do next. He couldn't keep pretending that he was fine, couldn't keep pushing Emma and Lily away, hiding his pain behind a mask of stoic silence. He had been trying to protect them, but in doing so, he had nearly destroyed them.

He needed to tell Emma—needed to be honest with her about how close he had come to leaving her, to leaving their daughter. The thought terrified him, but he knew that if he didn't confront it now, it would fester, growing into something even more dangerous. She deserved to know the truth, no matter how painful it was.

Jack sat there until the first light of dawn began to filter through the curtains, bathing the room in a soft, golden glow. It was a new day, and with it came a new resolve. He couldn't change what had happened, couldn't erase the pain he had caused or the fear that still gripped him. But he could take the first step toward making things right.

When Emma stirred awake a few hours later, she found Jack sitting at the kitchen table, a cup of coffee growing cold in front of him. The dark circles under his eyes, the tension in his shoulders—she knew something was wrong before he even spoke.

"Jack?" she asked, her voice thick with sleep and concern as she came over to him, placing a hand on his shoulder.

Jack looked up at her, his eyes red-rimmed and tired, and the words came tumbling out—an avalanche of pain, fear, and guilt that he had kept buried for far too long.

"I almost… I almost did something terrible last night," he began, his voice shaking. "Something I can't even begin to explain, but you need to know."

Emma's eyes widened, her hand tightening on his shoulder. "What are you talking about, Jack? What happened?"

Jack took a deep breath, forcing himself to hold her gaze. He owed her that much. "I almost took my own life,

Emma. I was sitting in the living room with the gun... I was ready to end it. I didn't see any other way out."

Emma's face drained of color, her breath hitching as she processed his words. She sank into the chair opposite him, her eyes filling with tears. "Jack, no... no..." she whispered, her voice breaking.

"I'm so sorry," Jack said, his voice trembling with emotion. "I've been so lost, so trapped in my own head, and I didn't see a way out. But then Lily... she saw me with the gun, and I realized what I was about to do to you, to her... I couldn't go through with it."

Emma's tears spilled over, and she reached out, grabbing his hands in hers. "Jack, you're scaring me... I knew you were struggling, but I didn't know it was this bad. Why didn't you tell me?"

Jack squeezed her hands, holding on like a lifeline. "I didn't want to burden you with all this. I thought I could handle it on my own, but I can't. I need help, Emma. Real help. I need to talk to someone—someone who can help me sort through all this before I do something I can't take back."

Emma nodded, her tears falling freely now. "We'll get through this, Jack. We'll find someone—whatever you need, we'll do it. You don't have to go through this alone."

For the first time in what felt like forever, Jack felt a glimmer of hope. It was faint, fragile, but it was there, like a light in the darkness that had consumed him for so long. He wasn't alone. Emma was here, and she wasn't giving up on him, even when he had nearly given up on himself.

"I'm sorry," he whispered again, the

weight of his apology pressing down on him. "I'm so sorry, Emma."

She shook her head, leaning across the table to pull him into a tight embrace. "Don't apologize, Jack. Just promise me you'll get the help you need. Promise me you won't give up."

"I promise," Jack said, his voice choked with emotion. "I won't give up. Not on you, not on Lily, not on myself."

They held each other for a long time, the morning light growing stronger as it filled the kitchen. Jack knew the road ahead would be long and difficult, but he was ready to take the first step. He had come too close to losing everything, and he wasn't about to let the darkness win.

With Emma by his side, he would fight his way back, no matter how long it took. He had to—because his life, their life together, was worth fighting for.

CHAPTER 5: REACHING OUT

The decision to seek help wasn't easy, and the days that followed were some of the hardest Jack had ever faced. He felt raw and exposed, like a wound that had been ripped open before it had a chance to heal. But he had made a promise to Emma, and to himself, that he would fight to find a way through the darkness that had almost consumed him.

Jack's first step was reaching out to Mike, a fellow veteran he had served with years ago. Mike had been through his own battles with PTSD and had come out the other side—scarred but still standing. Jack remembered how Mike had once mentioned a therapist who had helped him when he'd hit rock bottom. Jack didn't want to burden Emma with finding help for him; this was something he needed to do on his own.

He hesitated for a long time before picking up the phone, staring at Mike's number as if it were a bomb waiting to go off. Finally, with a deep breath, he dialed, each ring tightening the knot in his stomach. When Mike answered, his voice was warm and familiar, a lifeline in the darkness.

"Jack, man, it's been a while," Mike said, and Jack could hear the smile in his voice. "How've you been?"

Jack swallowed hard; his throat dry. "Not great, Mike. Not great at all."

There was a pause on the other end of the line, and Jack could almost hear the gears turning in Mike's head. "What's going on?" Mike asked, his tone shifting to one of concern. "You need to talk?"

Jack took a deep breath, forcing the

words out before he could change his mind. "I need help, Mike. I'm not okay, and I haven't been for a long time. I nearly... I nearly did something I can't take back."

Mike was silent for a moment, letting Jack's words sink in. When he spoke again, his voice was steady and serious. "I'm glad you called, Jack. You don't have to go through this alone, you know that, right?"

Jack nodded, even though Mike couldn't see him. "I know. It's just... hard to admit that I can't handle it on my own."

"It's not about handling it on your own," Mike said. "We all need help sometimes. There's no shame in that, man. You're still here, and that means you've got a chance to turn things around."

Jack felt a wave of relief at Mike's

words, as if a weight he had been carrying for months had suddenly lifted. "Do you still see that therapist you mentioned a while back? The one who helped you?"

"Yeah, I do," Mike replied. "Dr. Barnes. She's been a lifesaver for me, Jack. She gets it, you know? She's worked with a lot of vets, and she doesn't sugarcoat anything. She'll help you work through all the stuff that's eating you alive."

Jack felt a flicker of hope. "Do you think she'd be willing to take me on as a patient?"

"I don't see why not," Mike said. "I'll give you her contact info. Just tell her you're a friend of mine, and she'll take care of you."

Jack scribbled down the number Mike gave him, his hand shaking slightly as he did. It felt like a lifeline, a small, tangible step toward healing. He thanked Mike, and they talked a little longer—about their families, their lives since leaving the service—before hanging up. Jack felt a little lighter, as though the simple act of reaching out had begun to chip away at the walls he'd built around himself.

The next day, Jack called Dr. Barnes. He was nervous, his heart pounding as he waited for the receptionist to answer. But when she did, her voice was calm and reassuring, and Jack found himself scheduling an appointment for the following week. It was a small victory, but a victory nonetheless.

In the days leading up to his first session, Jack tried to keep himself busy. He spent more time with Emma and Lily, helping with chores around the house and taking Lily to the park. But the tension still hung in the air, a reminder that the darkness was never far away.

Emma was patient with him, offering quiet support without pushing him too hard. She seemed to sense that he needed to take this journey at his own pace, that he was fragile in a way she hadn't seen before. But there was also a new kind of closeness between them, a bond forged in the fire of the pain they had nearly lost each other to.

On the morning of his appointment, Jack woke up early, the anxiety gnawing at him like a wild animal. He hadn't told Emma about the appointment, not wanting to worry her until he was sure he could go through with it. As he got dressed, he caught a glimpse of himself in the mirror—his reflection seemed more solid now, more real, like he was slowly becoming grounded in his own life again.

The drive to Dr. Barnes' office felt like a

journey into the unknown. The streets were busy with morning traffic, but Jack barely noticed the cars around him. His mind was racing, filled with a mixture of dread and anticipation. He wasn't sure what to expect, wasn't sure how much he was ready to share. But he knew he had to try—he had to do this, not just for himself, but for his family.

Dr. Barnes' office was in a nondescript building on the outskirts of town. The waiting room was small and quiet, with soft lighting and comfortable chairs. Jack checked in at the front desk, then sat down, his hands clasped tightly in his lap. The minutes seemed to stretch on forever, each tick of the clock echoing in his head like a countdown to something he wasn't sure he was ready for.

Finally, the door to the inner office opened, and a woman in her late forties stepped out. She had short, silver-streaked hair and kind eyes that seemed to take in everything at once. She smiled when she saw him.

"Jack Reynolds?" she asked.

Jack nodded, standing up, feeling like a schoolboy called to the principal's office. "That's me."

"I'm Dr. Barnes," she said, extending her hand. Her grip was firm, reassuring. "It's nice to meet you. Come on in."

Jack followed her into the office, which was warm and inviting, with soft chairs and a window that let in plenty of natural light. Dr. Barnes gestured for him to sit, and he did, feeling awkward and out of place. This was foreign territory for him—talking about his feelings, about his experiences. He was used to keeping everything locked down, hidden away where no one could see.

Dr. Barnes sat across from him, her expression calm and open. She didn't have a notebook or a clipboard, just sat with her hands resting lightly in her lap, waiting for him to speak.

"How are you feeling today, Jack?" she asked after a moment.

Jack hesitated, the words caught in his throat. How could he even begin to describe what he was feeling? The fear, the guilt, the crushing weight of his memories? He took a deep breath, trying to steady himself.

"I'm... not great," he admitted, his voice quiet. "I've been struggling a lot since I got back. I... I almost did something really stupid."

Dr. Barnes nodded, her gaze steady.

"I'm glad you're here. Reaching out for help is the first step, and it's a big one."

Jack felt a lump form in his throat. "It doesn't feel like enough," he said, his voice trembling. "I don't know how to make it stop—the nightmares, the guilt. It's like I'm stuck in a loop, and I can't get out."

Dr. Barnes leaned forward slightly, her expression compassionate. "What you're feeling is something a lot of veterans experience, Jack. You've been through things that most people can't even imagine, and those experiences have left deep scars. But those scars don't have to define you. We can work through this, one step at a time."

Jack nodded, though he still felt a deep sense of uncertainty. "I don't know where to start," he admitted, his voice small.

"We'll start wherever you're comfortable," Dr. Barnes said gently. "This is your space, Jack. There's no rush, no pressure. We'll take it at your pace."

The session passed in a blur. Jack found himself talking more than he had expected—about the nightmares, the memories that haunted him, the fear that he was losing himself. Dr. Barnes listened without judgment, offering insights that made him see his experiences in a new light.

By the time the session ended, Jack felt drained but also lighter, as if a small part of the weight he'd been carrying had been lifted. Dr. Barnes scheduled another appointment for the following week, and Jack left the office feeling a mix of exhaustion and hope. It was just the beginning, but it was a beginning.

When Jack returned home, Emma was

waiting for him in the kitchen, a cup of coffee in hand. She looked up as he walked in, her eyes filled with concern and curiosity.

"How did it go?" she asked, her voice tentative.

Jack smiled, though it was small and weary. "It was... good," he said, surprising himself with the honesty of the answer. "It's going to be a long road, but I think I'm ready to start walking it."

Emma's eyes softened with relief, and she set the coffee down, stepping forward to pull him into a hug. "I'm proud of you, Jack," she whispered, her voice thick with emotion."

"You don't know how much this means to me."

Jack held her close, absorbing the warmth of her embrace. For the first time in what felt like forever, he allowed himself to lean into her support without feeling guilty or ashamed. It was a small moment of peace, but it was real, and he held onto it as if it were the only thing keeping him from drifting away.

Over the next few weeks, Jack continued his sessions with Dr. Barnes. Each appointment was grueling, forcing him to confront parts of himself that he had long kept buried. He talked about the village, about the faces of the civilians that haunted his dreams, about the crushing weight of guilt that had driven him to the brink. It was painful, like tearing open an old wound, but with each session, he felt the tiniest sliver of relief, as though the poison was slowly being drawn out.

Dr. Barnes helped him understand that what he was experiencing was not just PTSD but something deeper—moral injury. It was a term Jack had never heard before, but it resonated with him. Moral injury was the damage done to one's conscience when they perpetrate, witness, or fail to prevent acts that transgress their moral beliefs. For Jack, it wasn't just about the trauma of war; it was about the profound sense of having violated something sacred within himself.

"Your guilt is real and valid," Dr. Barnes explained during one session. "But it's not something you have to carry alone. You were put in an impossible situation, and you did the best you could with the information you had at the time. The fact that you feel this guilt shows that you are a person of deep conscience. But that doesn't mean you have to let it destroy you."

Jack sat quietly, absorbing her words. He had never thought of his guilt in that way—had never considered that it might be a sign of his humanity rather than his failure. The idea gave him something to hold onto, a small piece of understanding amid the chaos that still churned inside him.

One day, after a particularly difficult session, Jack found himself driving aimlessly through town, the familiar streets passing by in a blur. He wasn't sure where he was going until he found himself pulling into the parking lot of the local VFW hall. It was a place he had avoided since his return, not wanting to be around others who might remind him of the life he was trying to escape. But today, something drew him there, a need to connect with others who might understand what he was going through.

The hall was quiet when he entered, the smell of old wood and stale coffee filling the air. A few veterans sat scattered around the room, talking quietly in groups or sitting alone, lost in thought.

Jack hesitated in the doorway, feeling out of place and unsure if he belonged here. But something in him pushed him forward, a small voice reminding him that he couldn't do this alone.

He spotted a familiar face at one of the tables—an older man named Tom, who had served in Vietnam and had been a fixture at the VFW for as long as Jack could remember. Tom had always been friendly, offering a kind word or a piece of advice to the younger veterans who wandered in. Jack had spoken to him a few times before his last deployment but had avoided him since coming back, not ready to face the questions and concern he knew Tom would have.

But today, Jack felt different. He felt ready, or at least willing, to try and talk about what was going on inside him. He walked over to the table where Tom was sitting and offered a small nod.

"Mind if I join you?" Jack asked, his voice tentative.

Tom looked up, his weathered face breaking into a smile. "Jack, good to see you, son. Sit down, sit down. It's been a while."

Jack slid into the chair across from Tom, feeling awkward but relieved to be there. He wasn't sure how to start, how to explain the mess of emotions that had driven him to this point, but Tom didn't seem to be in any rush. He just sat there, his gaze steady and patient, waiting for Jack to speak.

After a few moments of silence, Jack finally found his voice. "I'm not doing so well, Tom," he admitted, his voice low. "It's been rough since I got back. I've been trying to handle it on my own, but... it's not working."

Tom nodded, his expression

understanding. "It's tough, Jack. Coming back home isn't always easy, especially when you've seen the things you've seen. I've been where you are. Hell, I think we all have at some point."

Jack looked down at his hands, the words he wanted to say jumbled up inside him. "I've been going to therapy," he said after a pause. "It's helping, but... I don't know, I still feel like I'm drowning."

Tom leaned back in his chair, taking a sip of his coffee. "Therapy's good. It helps you make sense of things, gives you tools to cope. But sometimes, it's the connection with others that really pulls you out of the deep end. Talking to people who've been through the same kind of hell you have—it helps."

Jack nodded slowly, feeling a flicker of hope. "I think that's why I came here today. I've been so caught up in my own head that I've pushed everyone away. But I don't want to do that anymore. I don't want to be alone with this."

Tom smiled, a warm and reassuring expression. "You're not alone, Jack. We're all in this together. Anytime you need to talk, you know where to find me. And if you ever want to share your story, we're here to listen. No judgment, no pressure—just support."

Jack felt a lump form in his throat, the weight of his isolation slowly lifting. For the first time in a long time, he felt like he belonged somewhere, like there were people who understood the darkness he was fighting against.

"Thanks, Tom," Jack said quietly. "That means a lot."

They sat in companionable silence for a while, sipping their coffee and watching the other veterans move around the hall. Jack felt a sense of calm that had been absent for months, a peace that came from knowing he didn't have to carry his burden alone. There were others who had walked this path before him, who had faced their demons and come out the other side. If they could do it, maybe he could too.

As the afternoon wore on, more veterans trickled into the hall, some joining Jack and Tom at their table. They talked about their lives, their struggles, and their victories, sharing stories that were both painful and healing. Jack listened more than he spoke, but for the first time, he felt like he was truly part of something—a brotherhood that didn't end when the uniform came off.

When he finally left the VFW hall that evening, the sun was beginning to set, casting a warm golden light over the town. Jack took a deep breath, feeling more grounded than he had in months. He knew the road ahead was still long and uncertain, but for the first time, he didn't feel like he was walking it alone.

Back at home, Emma was waiting for him on the porch, her face lighting up when she saw him. "How was it?" she asked, standing to greet him as he walked up the steps.

"It was good," Jack replied, his voice steady. "Really good. I think it was exactly what I needed."

Emma smiled; relief evident in her eyes. "I'm so glad, Jack. I've been worried about you."

"I know," Jack said, reaching out to take her hand. "But I think I'm finally starting to find my way back. It's not going to be easy, but I'm ready to try."

They stood there for a moment, holding

hands and watching the sun dip below the horizon. The sky was a wash of colors—orange, pink, and purple—and for the first time in a long while, Jack allowed himself to appreciate its beauty.

"Let's go inside," Emma said softly, squeezing his hand. "Lily's waiting for you."

Jack nodded, feeling a deep sense of gratitude for his family, for their unwavering support and love. He knew he still had a long way to go, but with Emma and Lily by his side, and with the support of people like Tom, he felt like he could face whatever challenges lay ahead.

As they walked into the house, the warmth of home enveloped him, and for the first time since his return, Jack felt a flicker of hope—real, tangible hope—that things could get better. He wasn't alone, and he wasn't beyond saving.

The road ahead would be difficult, but he was ready to walk it, one step at a time.

And that, Jack realized, was enough.

CHAPTER 6: THE BURDEN OF GUILT

Despite the small victories, the sense of community at the VFW hall, and the growing closeness with his family, Jack's burden of guilt remained a constant companion. It was a heavy, invisible weight that pressed on his chest, making it hard to breathe, hard to think, hard to believe that he deserved any of the good things that had started to come his way. Each night, as he lay in bed, he replayed the events of the raid in his mind, the same relentless loop of memories that refused to let him go.

During his sessions with Dr. Barnes, Jack had begun to understand the concept of moral injury in greater depth. It wasn't just the trauma of war that haunted him; it was the profound sense that he had violated his own moral code, that he had become someone he didn't recognize. The people who had died under his command—the civilians, the innocents—were like ghosts that clung to him, reminders of what he had done and what he could never undo.

Dr. Barnes encouraged Jack to talk about the raid, to recount it in detail, to face the memories head-on rather than trying to bury them. But each time he tried, the words stuck in his throat, the images flashing in his mind too vivid, too painful. He wanted to speak, to let it all out, but the guilt was a living thing inside him, strangling the words before they could escape.

One afternoon, after a particularly difficult session, Jack drove to a nearby park. It was the kind of place he might have taken Lily if he were in a better state of mind—filled with children playing, families picnicking, the sounds of laughter and joy. But today, the noise grated on him, a painful contrast to the darkness that swirled inside his head. He found a secluded bench at the edge of the park, away from the happy chaos, and sat down heavily.

He took out his phone, scrolling through his contacts until he found Mike's number. His thumb hovered over the call button, but he couldn't bring himself to press it. Mike had been a lifeline, but there were things even Mike didn't know, things Jack wasn't sure he could ever share. Instead, he slipped the phone back into his pocket and leaned forward, resting his head in his hands.

The sound of children playing nearby brought a surge of guilt so intense that it made Jack's stomach churn. He thought about the kids in that village— the ones who hadn't made it out alive, who had been caught in the crossfire because of his orders. He could see their faces so clearly, could hear the screams, could feel the terror in the air as the raid spiraled out of control.

It wasn't supposed to go down like that. They had gone in believing they were targeting an insurgent stronghold, based on intelligence they'd trusted. But the intel had been wrong, disastrously wrong, and by the time they realized it, it was too late. Jack had given the order to engage, had sent his men in with the expectation that they were fighting the enemy, only to find out too late that they had made a grave mistake.

He had tried to call off the assault, but the chaos, the confusion—it had all happened so fast. Shots were fired, and before he knew it, innocent people were lying in the dirt, bleeding out because of decisions he had made. He could still see the young boy who had died in his arms, his blood staining Jack's uniform, the light fading from his eyes as Jack whispered apologies that the boy couldn't understand.

Jack clenched his fists, his nails digging into his palms, trying to ground himself in the present, but the memories were too strong. He had killed that boy as surely as if he had pulled the trigger himself, and no amount of therapy or talking could change that. It was a fact, a truth that he would carry with him until the day he died.

The sound of a child's laughter nearby brought him back to the present with a jolt. Jack looked up, blinking back tears he hadn't realized were there. A little girl, no older than Lily, was playing on the swings, her father pushing her gently, her giggles filling the air. It was an innocent, beautiful moment, and it made Jack's heart ache with a longing he couldn't describe.

He wanted so badly to be that father—to be the man who could laugh and play with his daughter without the weight of his past crushing him. But every time he looked at Lily, he saw the faces of the children who had died, saw the boy in the village, and the guilt nearly tore him apart.

Jack leaned back on the bench, closing his eyes, trying to will the memories away. But they were always there, lurking just beneath the surface, ready to strike the moment he let his guard down. He couldn't escape them, couldn't forget what he had done. And that, more than anything, was what made the guilt so unbearable—it was inescapable, unrelenting.

Dr. Barnes had told him that guilt could be a double-edged sword. On one hand, it was a sign of his conscience, a testament to the fact that he cared deeply about the lives he had taken. But on the other hand, if left unchecked, it could consume him, destroy him from the inside out. She had encouraged him to find ways to channel that guilt into something positive, to use it as a force for good rather than letting it drag him down.

But Jack didn't know how to do that. How could he turn something so dark, so heavy, into anything good? How could he ever atone for the lives he had taken, for the pain he had caused? It felt like an impossible task, one that was far beyond his reach.

The sound of footsteps approaching pulled Jack out of his thoughts. He opened his eyes to see an elderly man walking toward him, a gentle smile on his face. The man was dressed simply, in jeans and a flannel shirt, his white hair combed neatly to the side. He looked familiar, but Jack couldn't quite place him.

"Mind if I sit?" the man asked, gesturing to the empty spot on the bench beside Jack.

Jack shook his head, grateful for the distraction. "Go ahead."

The man sat down slowly, sighing as he settled in. He glanced over at the children playing in the park, a look of contentment on his face. "Beautiful day isn't it?"

"Yeah," Jack replied, though he wasn't sure he believed it.

The man nodded, as if sensing Jack's unease. "I've seen you here a few times before. You look like you've got a lot on your mind."

Jack stiffened, not sure how to respond. He hadn't realized anyone had noticed him, let alone someone who had seen him more than once. "I guess you could say that" he said cautiously.

The man chuckled softly. "I'm not trying to pry, son. Just making conversation. I know that look, though. Seen it before in a lot of guys who come back from places no one should have to go."

Jack glanced at the man, suddenly realizing why he seemed familiar. "You were in the service?" he asked, though it was more of a statement than a question.

The man nodded. "Korea. Long time ago now, but some things never leave you, no matter how much time passes."

Jack felt a strange sense of kinship with the man, though they were generations apart. "Did you… did you ever feel like you couldn't move past it? Like the things you did over there would follow you forever?"

The man was quiet for a moment, as if considering how to answer. When he spoke, his voice was gentle, but there was a deep sadness in it. "Yeah, I felt that way. Still do sometimes. There are things I saw, things I did... They stick with you. But I've learned that it's not about forgetting. It's about finding a way to live with it, to make peace with the choices you made, even when those choices haunt you."

Jack stared at the ground, the man's words hitting him hard. "But how do you make peace with it when the guilt is so strong? How do you forgive yourself for something you can never take back?"

The man sighed, leaning back on the bench. "Forgiveness is a tricky thing, Jack. It's not just about letting go of what you did; it's about accepting that you're human, that you did the best you could in a situation where there were no good options. Sometimes, all you can do is make amends in the ways that are available to you and try to live the rest of your life in a way that honors those you've lost."

Jack felt a lump form in his throat, the man's words resonating with him on a level he hadn't expected. "I don't know if I can do that," he admitted, his voice barely above a whisper.

The man looked at Jack, his expression kind but firm. "It's not something you do overnight. It's a process, one that takes time, patience, and a lot of work. But it starts with one simple step—accepting that you're still here, that you still have the power to make a difference, even if it's just in small ways."

Jack thought about what the man had

said, about the idea of making amends. It wasn't something he had considered before, not really. He had been so focused on the guilt, on the weight of his actions, that he hadn't thought about how he could use that guilt to drive him toward something positive, something that might bring a little light into the darkness.

"Thank you," Jack said quietly, looking at the man with a newfound sense of gratitude.

The man smiled gently, his eyes reflecting a lifetime of experience and understanding. "You're welcome, son. Remember, you're not alone in this. There are others who've been where you are, who've felt what you're feeling. And there's always a way forward, even when it feels like there isn't."

Jack nodded, absorbing the man's words. For the first time, the idea of making amends didn't seem like an insurmountable task. It was daunting, yes, but the man's calm assurance gave Jack a glimmer of hope—a sense that maybe, just maybe, he could find a way to live with the guilt instead of being consumed by it.

The two men sat in silence for a few more minutes, watching the children play in the park. Jack found himself focusing on the sound of their laughter, the innocence in their voices. It was a reminder of what he had lost and what he still had—a chance to be present for his own daughter, to protect her innocence and give her the father she deserved.

As the man stood to leave, he placed a reassuring hand on Jack's shoulder. "Take care of yourself, Jack. And remember, it's never too late to start healing."

Jack looked up, meeting the man's

gaze. "I'll try," he said, his voice steady. "Thanks again... for everything."

The man nodded and walked away, leaving Jack alone with his thoughts. He watched as the man disappeared into the crowd, feeling a strange mixture of sadness and resolve. The conversation had stirred something deep within him, something he hadn't felt in a long time—a desire to take control of his life, to start making decisions that would lead him out of the darkness instead of deeper into it.

Jack sat on the bench for a while longer, lost in thought. The guilt was still there, a heavy presence in his chest, but it didn't feel as overwhelming as before. It was as if the man's words had given him a roadmap—a way to navigate through the pain and find a path toward some semblance of peace.

He thought about what the man had

said about making amends. What could he do to honor the lives that had been lost? How could he turn his guilt into something positive, something that would help him move forward? The questions swirled in his mind, but for the first time, they didn't feel like a burden. They felt like a challenge, a call to action.

Jack realized that he didn't have to do this alone. He had Emma, he had Lily, and he had people like Dr. Barnes and the veterans at the VFW who understood what he was going through. And maybe, just maybe, he could find a way to honor the memories of those who had died by living his life in a way that made their loss mean something.

With a newfound sense of purpose, Jack stood up from the bench, feeling a little lighter. He wasn't sure what the future held, but he knew he couldn't keep running from his past. It was time to face it, to confront the darkness head-on and start the long, difficult process of healing.

As he walked back to his car, Jack decided. He would talk to Dr. Barnes about how he could start making amends—how he could channel his guilt into something constructive. Maybe it was through volunteering, or helping other veterans, or simply being the best father and husband he could be. Whatever it was, he knew he needed to find it, to embrace it, and to use it as a way to move forward.

When Jack got home that evening, he found Emma and Lily in the living room, playing a board game together. Lily looked up and smiled when she saw him, her face lighting up with pure, unfiltered joy.

"Daddy, come play with us!" she called, waving him over.

Jack felt a pang of guilt as he looked at his daughter, but he also felt something else—hope. The man's words echoed in his mind: It's never too late to start healing.

He walked over to the table, sitting down beside Lily and pulling her into a hug. She giggled, wrapping her arms around his neck and giving him a squeeze.

"Missed you today, Daddy," she said, her voice muffled against his shirt.

Jack kissed the top of her head, his heart swelling with love and gratitude. "I missed you too, sweetheart," he replied, his voice thick with emotion. "I'm here now, and I'm not going anywhere."

Emma watched them with a soft smile, her eyes filled with warmth. Jack met her gaze, and in that moment, he knew he was making the right choice. He wasn't going to let the guilt control him anymore. He was going to find a way to live with it, to honor the past while building a future for himself and his family.

"Let's play," Jack said, releasing Lily and turning his attention to the game on the table. "I'm ready to take you both on."

Lily laughed, her eyes sparkling with excitement. "You're going down, Daddy!"

As they played, Jack felt a sense of peace settle over him. It wasn't complete—there was still a long road ahead, filled with challenges and setbacks. But for the first time in a long while, he felt like he was on the right path. He was surrounded by love, by the people who mattered most to him, and he was ready to fight for them, to fight for himself.

When the game ended and Lily was tucked into bed, Jack and Emma sat together on the porch, watching the stars twinkle in the night sky. The air was cool, and the world felt quiet and still, as if it were holding its breath, waiting for something.

"How was your day?" Emma asked, her voice soft as she leaned against him.

"It was… different," Jack replied, choosing his words carefully. "I met someone at the park. An older guy, a veteran. He helped me see things a little more clearly."

Emma looked up at him, her eyes filled with curiosity. "What did he say?"

Jack took a deep breath, remembering the conversation. "He told me that it's not about forgetting what happened. It's about finding a way to live with it, to make peace with the choices I made, even if they haunt me. He said I need to find a way to make amends, to use my guilt for something good."

Emma squeezed his hand, her expression tender. "That sounds like good advice."

"It is," Jack agreed, his voice steady. "And I think... I think I'm ready to start doing that. I don't know exactly how yet, but I want to figure it out. I want to find a way to honor the people I couldn't save, to live in a way that would make them proud."

Emma's eyes filled with tears, but she smiled, a bright, beautiful smile that made Jack's heart ache with love. "I'm so proud of you, Jack. And whatever you decide to do, I'll be right here with you. We'll get through this together."

Jack wrapped his arm around her, pulling her close as they sat in the quiet of the night. The stars above them were like tiny beacons of light, guiding them forward, one small step at a time.

And for the first time, Jack felt like he could see a future for himself—a future where the past didn't define him, where he could find peace and redemption. It wouldn't be easy, and there would be days when the darkness would try to pull him back under. But he knew now that he didn't have to face it alone.

With Emma by his side and a renewed sense of purpose, Jack was ready to take on the challenge, to face his guilt and turn it into something that could help him heal. It was a long road ahead, but he was no longer afraid to walk it. He was ready to start healing, to start living again.

CHAPTER 7: STEPS TOWARD HEALING

In the weeks that followed, Jack began to take small but significant steps toward healing. Each day was a struggle, but he was committed to the promise he had made—to himself, to Emma, and to the memory of those he had lost. The road was long and difficult, but with each step, he began to feel a little more like himself, a little more in control of his life.

One of the first things Jack did was return to the VFW hall. He started attending regularly, not just as a visitor but as an active participant. He shared more of his story, opening up about the guilt and the nightmares, about the moment he had nearly taken his own life. It wasn't easy—each word felt like dragging a boulder up a hill—but the support he received from the other veterans was like a balm to his wounded soul.

Tom, the older veteran he had met in the park, became a regular companion at these meetings. They often sat together, talking long after the official gatherings had ended. Tom's steady presence and quiet wisdom gave Jack a sense of stability, a reminder that it was possible to carry the weight of the past without being crushed by it.

One evening, after a particularly intense meeting where Jack had shared more than he ever thought he could, Tom suggested something that took Jack by surprise.

"You ever thought about doing some volunteer work, Jack?" Tom asked as they walked out of the hall together.

Jack frowned, unsure where the question was leading. "Volunteer work?

Like what?"

Tom shrugged, lighting a cigarette as they walked. "There's a lot of ways to give back, you know. Some of the guys here volunteer with local youth groups, others help out at shelters, or work with disabled vets. It helps to have something to focus on, something that takes you outside of your own head."

Jack thought about it, the idea rolling around in his mind. "I don't know if I'm ready for that," he admitted. "I'm still trying to get my own life in order."

"That's exactly why it might be good for you," Tom said, exhaling a puff of smoke. "Helping others can be a way of helping yourself. It gives you a sense of purpose, something positive to focus on. And it might help you start to forgive yourself a little, knowing you're making a difference."

Jack was silent for a moment, considering Tom's words. The idea of volunteering had never crossed his mind. He had been so focused on his own pain that he hadn't thought about how he could use his experiences to help others. But the more he thought about it, the more it made sense.

"I'll think about it," Jack said finally, nodding to himself. "Maybe you're right. Maybe it's time to start doing something that helps someone else."

Tom smiled, clapping Jack on the back. "That's the spirit. Let me know if you want to get involved in anything. I can introduce you to some folks who could use a hand."

The idea stayed with Jack as he drove home that night. He thought about the possibilities, about the different ways he could give back. He didn't know where to start, but he was willing to try.

It felt like another small step toward redemption, another way to make amends for the things he had done.

The next day, Jack mentioned the idea to Emma as they sat together at the kitchen table, drinking their morning coffee. The light of dawn filtered through the window, casting a warm glow over the room, and for the first time in a long while, Jack felt a sense of hope.

"Tom suggested I get involved in some volunteer work," Jack said, keeping his tone casual, though the idea filled him with both excitement and anxiety. "He thinks it might help me, you know, find some purpose."

Emma looked up from her coffee, her eyes bright with interest. "I think that's a great idea, Jack. It could be really good for you, and for the people you'd be helping."

Jack nodded, taking a sip of his coffee. "Yeah, I think so too. I just... I'm not sure where to start. There are so many options, and I don't know what I'd be good at."

Emma reached across the table, taking his hand in hers. "You don't have to figure it all out at once. Just start small. Maybe talk to some of the other veterans, see what they're involved in. You'll find something that feels right."

Jack squeezed her hand, grateful for her support. "Thanks, Em. I don't know what I'd do without you."

Emma smiled, her eyes softening with love. "You don't have to do anything without me, Jack. We're in this together, remember?"

Jack smiled back, the warmth of her words filling him with a renewed sense of determination. He had been given a second chance, and he wasn't going to waste it. He was going to find a way to turn his pain into something meaningful, something that could help others, and maybe—just maybe—help himself in the process.

Over the next few weeks, Jack started exploring different volunteer opportunities. He talked to Tom and some of the other veterans at the VFW, learning about the various ways they were giving back to the community. One veteran, a woman named Sarah who had served in Iraq, told Jack about a local organization that worked with homeless veterans, helping them find housing, jobs, and mental health support.

"They're always looking for volunteers," Sarah said, handing Jack a flyer. "You don't need any special skills, just a willingness to help. A lot of these guys are just like us—they've been through hell, and they need someone who understands."

Jack looked at the flyer, feeling a stir of interest. "I think I'd like to check it out," he said. "It sounds like something I could really get behind."

Sarah smiled, nodding in approval. "They meet every Saturday morning. Why don't you come with me this weekend? I can introduce you to the team."

Jack agreed, and that Saturday, he found himself standing outside a small, unassuming building on the edge of town. The sign above the door read "Veterans Outreach Center," and the parking lot was filled with cars, a sign that the organization was busy and active.

Sarah met him at the door, her smile

warm and welcoming. "Glad you could make it," she said, leading him inside. "Let me introduce you to some of the folks here."

The interior of the building was simple but inviting, with a reception area, a few offices, and a large common room where volunteers and veterans gathered. The atmosphere was one of camaraderie and support, and Jack felt a sense of ease as he was introduced to the staff and other volunteers.

One of the team leaders, a middle-aged man named Greg, welcomed Jack with a firm handshake. "We're always happy to have new volunteers," Greg said, his tone friendly. "There's a lot of work to be done, and every bit helps."

Greg gave Jack a quick tour of the facility, explaining the different programs they offered. There was a food pantry, a clothing donation center, and a job placement service, all geared toward helping veterans get back on their feet. Jack was impressed by the scope of the work being done and felt a growing sense of excitement about getting involved.

By the end of the tour, Jack had agreed to start volunteering with the job placement program, helping veterans write resumes, prepare for interviews, and connect with potential employers. It was a role that felt meaningful and tangible, a way for Jack to use his skills to make a real difference in the lives of others.

Over the next few months, Jack threw himself into the work at the Veterans Outreach Center. He spent every Saturday morning at the center, meeting with veterans, listening to their stories, and helping them take the next steps toward rebuilding their lives. The work was challenging, but it was also incredibly rewarding. For the first time in a long time, Jack felt like he was making a positive impact, like he was giving back in a way that honored the lives of those who had been lost.

Through his volunteer work, Jack began to see the strength and resilience of the veterans he was helping. Many of them had faced unimaginable hardships—combat, homelessness, addiction—but they were still fighting, still pushing forward. Their determination inspired Jack, gave him hope that he, too, could find a way through the darkness.

As Jack spent more time at the center, he also began to open up more in his therapy sessions with Dr. Barnes. He talked about the guilt, the nightmares, and the fear that he would never be able to forgive himself. But he also talked about the progress he was making, the sense of purpose he was finding through his volunteer work, and the small moments of peace that were becoming more frequent.

"You're doing incredible work, Jack," Dr. Barnes said during one session, her voice full of encouragement. "You're turning your pain into something positive, and that's no small feat. But remember, it's okay to acknowledge the progress you've made. Healing is a journey, not a destination. You're allowed to feel good about the steps you've taken."

Jack nodded, feeling a sense of pride that he hadn't allowed himself to feel before. "It's still hard," he admitted. "There are days when the guilt feels overwhelming, when I wonder if I'll ever be able to fully move past it. But I'm starting to see that maybe I don't have to move past it. Maybe I just need to find a way to live with it, to carry it with me in a way that doesn't destroy me."

Dr. Barnes smiled, her expression full of warmth. "That's exactly right, Jack. The guilt doesn't have to be a weight that drags you down. It can be a driving force that propels you forward. It can remind you of the person you are now, the person you want to be, and help you make decisions that align with those values. It's not about erasing the past; it's about integrating it into your present in a way that allows you to live a full and meaningful life."

Jack considered her words, realizing the truth in them. For so long, he had been trying to push the guilt away, to pretend it didn't exist, or to drown it in alcohol. But now, he was learning that the guilt didn't have to define him. It was a part of him, yes, but it didn't have to consume him. He could use it to guide his actions, to remind himself of the importance of living with integrity, compassion, and purpose.

As the weeks turned into months, Jack continued to make progress. The nightmares still came, but they were less frequent, and when they did, he found that he could talk about them with Emma or Dr. Barnes, rather than bottling them up inside. He started to feel more present in his day-to-day life, more engaged with Emma and Lily, more at peace with himself.

One Saturday, after a particularly busy morning at the Veterans Outreach Center, Jack was getting ready to leave when Greg, the team leader, approached him with a smile.

"Jack, I wanted to talk to you about something," Greg said, his tone serious but friendly. "You've been doing incredible work here, and the veterans you've been helping have nothing but good things to say about you. We've been thinking about expanding our job placement program, and I was wondering if you'd be interested in taking on a larger role, maybe helping to lead the program."

Jack was taken aback. He had never considered himself a leader, especially not in the state he had been in just a few months ago. But the work he was doing at the center had given him a sense of purpose he hadn't felt in a long time. The idea of taking on more responsibility, of helping even more veterans, was both daunting and exciting.

"Wow, Greg, I'm honored," Jack said, trying to process the offer. "I'd love to help in any way I can, but are you sure I'm the right person for the job? I'm still figuring things out myself."

Greg smiled, clapping Jack on the shoulder. "That's exactly why you're the right person. You've been where these guys are, you understand what they're going through, and you're committed to making a difference. You've shown incredible dedication, and I think you'd be a great leader for this program."

Jack felt a swell of pride and gratitude. For so long, he had doubted his own worth, questioned whether he could ever be anything more than the sum of his mistakes. But now, standing amid people who believed in him, who saw his potential, he realized that maybe he could be more. Maybe he could use his experiences to help others find their way, just as he had started to find his.

"I'd be honored to take on the role," Jack said, his voice steady. "Thank you for believing in me, Greg."

Greg nodded, a satisfied smile on his face. "The honor's ours, Jack. I know you're going to do great things here."

As Jack drove home that afternoon, he felt a deep sense of fulfillment, something he hadn't felt in a long time. He had spent so many months lost in the darkness of his guilt, drowning in the memories of the past, but now he was starting to see a way forward. He was starting to see that his life could have meaning, that he could make a difference, not just for himself, but for others who were struggling as he had.

When he arrived home, Emma was in the kitchen, preparing dinner while Lily colored at the table. The house was filled with the warm, comforting smells of cooking, and the sound of Lily's laughter echoed through the room. Jack stood in the doorway for a moment, taking it all in, feeling a wave of love and gratitude wash over him.

He walked over to Emma, wrapping his arms around her from behind and kissing the top of her head. She leaned back into him, a smile spreading across her face.

"You're in a good mood," she said, her voice teasing. "Did something happen at the center today?"

Jack nodded, his heart swelling with pride. "Yeah, something did. Greg asked me to take on a leadership role in the job placement program. He thinks I'd be good at it, that I could help more veterans if I stepped up."

Emma turned in his arms, her eyes shining with pride. "Jack, that's amazing! I'm so proud of you."

Jack smiled, pulling her close. "I'm proud of me too," he admitted, the words feeling foreign but right. "For the first time in a long time, I feel like I'm actually doing something that matters. Like I'm making a difference."

Emma reached up, cupping his face in her hands. "You've always made a difference, Jack. But now you're starting to see it too. And that's what matters."

Jack kissed her, feeling a sense of peace and contentment that had eluded him for so long. When he pulled back, he saw Lily watching them, a curious expression on her face.

"Daddy, why are you and Mommy smiling so much?" she asked, her head tilted to the side.

Jack laughed, walking over to her and scooping her up into his arms. "Because we're happy, sweetheart. We're happy because we love each other, and because we have you."

Lily giggled, wrapping her arms around Jack's neck. "I love you too, Daddy."

Jack held her close, his heart full. In that moment, he realized just how far he had come, how much he had to be grateful for. The road ahead was still long, and there would be challenges, but he knew now that he could face them. He wasn't alone—he had his family, his friends, and a newfound sense of purpose to guide him.

As they sat down to dinner that night, Jack looked around the table at the people he loved most in the world. He had been to the edge and back, and while the scars would always be there, he knew they didn't define him. What defined him was the choice he made every day to keep going, to keep fighting, to keep living.

And for the first time in a long while, Jack felt truly hopeful about the future. He was healing, step by step, and he knew that as long as he kept moving forward, there was nothing he couldn't overcome.

CHAPTER 8: A NEW BATTLE

Jack's life had begun to regain some semblance of normalcy. The routine of working at the Veterans Outreach Center, spending time with his family, and continuing his therapy sessions provided a structure that helped him feel anchored. But despite the progress he had made, Jack knew that healing wasn't a straight path. The peace he had found was fragile, and it didn't take much to shatter it.

It happened on an otherwise ordinary afternoon. Jack was finishing up a session at the Outreach Center when his phone buzzed in his pocket. He glanced at the screen and saw Mike's name flashing. A cold feeling settled in his gut. Mike didn't usually call during the day. Jack excused himself and stepped outside to take the call, the crisp autumn air biting against his skin.

"Hey, Mike. What's up?" Jack asked, trying to keep his tone light.

There was a pause on the other end of the line, just long enough for Jack to feel the hairs on the back of his neck stand up.

"It's about Luis," Mike said, his voice low and strained.

Luis had been in their unit, one of the good guys—always quick with a joke, always willing to help out. He had been struggling since they got back, more than most, but he was tough. He was a fighter.

"What happened?" Jack asked, though he already knew. He could hear it in Mike's voice.

"He's gone, Jack. Took his own life last night."

The words hit Jack like a physical blow. He staggered back, leaning against the brick wall of the building as the world spun around him. He heard Mike's voice, distant and distorted, trying to explain what had happened, but the details didn't matter. All Jack could focus on was that Luis, the man who had stood beside him in battle, was gone.

"Jack? You still there?" Mike's voice cut through the haze.

"Yeah," Jack said, his voice hollow. "I'm here."

"They found him in his apartment. His sister's the one who found him. She's devastated. The funeral's in a few days… I thought you'd want to know."

Jack closed his eyes, a wave of nausea washing over him. He had been so focused on his own healing, on trying to put the pieces of his life back together, that he hadn't been paying attention to the others who were still struggling. He should have reached out to Luis, should have done more to make sure he was okay. But he hadn't, and now it was too late.

"Thanks for telling me, Mike," Jack said, struggling to keep his voice steady. "I... I'll be there."

They exchanged a few more words, but Jack barely registered them. When the call ended, he stood there for a long time, staring at his phone as if it held some kind of answer. But there were no answers, only the cold, hard reality that another one of his brothers was gone.

Jack drove home in a daze, his mind racing with thoughts he couldn't control. He replayed every interaction he'd had with Luis since they returned home, searching for signs he might have missed, moments when he could have stepped in and done something—anything—to change the outcome. But all he could see was the finality of it, the irrevocable loss.

When he walked through the front door, Emma immediately sensed that something was wrong. She was in the kitchen, preparing dinner, and the look of concern on her face deepened as soon as she saw him.

"Jack? What happened?" she asked, setting down the knife she was using to chop vegetables and walking over to him.

Jack stared at her, his eyes unfocused, his mind still trying to process the news. "Luis… he's gone," he said, his voice cracking. "He killed himself."

Emma's hand flew to her mouth, her

eyes wide with shock. "Oh my God, Jack... I'm so sorry."

She reached out, pulling him into a tight embrace, and Jack let her hold him, his body trembling with a mix of grief and guilt. He had thought he was making progress, thought he was finally finding his way out of the darkness, but this—this felt like a setback he wasn't sure he could recover from.

"I should have done something," Jack murmured, his voice muffled against Emma's shoulder. "I should have known he was struggling. I should have helped him."

"You can't blame yourself," Emma said gently, though her voice was thick with emotion. "You've been through so much, Jack. You can't take on the responsibility for everyone else's pain."

"But I wasn't there for him," Jack

insisted, pulling back to look at her. "I was so focused on myself, on trying to get better, that I didn't think about the others who were still hurting. I let him down, Emma. I let him down, and now he's gone."

Emma's eyes filled with tears, and she cupped his face in her hands, her touch warm and grounding. "Jack, listen to me. You are not responsible for this. Luis made his own choices, just like you made yours. You've done everything you can to heal, to help others, but you can't save everyone. No one can."

Jack wanted to believe her, wanted to let go of the guilt that was tearing him apart, but it wasn't that simple. The weight of Luis's death pressed down on him, suffocating him, and no matter how hard he tried to fight it, he couldn't shake the feeling that he had failed his friend.

The next few days passed in a blur. Jack went through the motions—getting up, going to work, spending time with Emma and Lily—but his heart wasn't in it. He felt numb, disconnected from everything and everyone around him. The progress he had made seemed to unravel, the darkness creeping back in, whispering that he would never be free of the guilt, that he would never be able to escape the past.

The day of Luis's funeral was cold and overcast, the sky heavy with gray clouds that threatened rain. Jack dressed in his best suit; the same one he had worn to so many other funerals, and drove to the church where the service was being held. The parking lot was filled with cars, and Jack recognized many of the faces as he walked inside—men and women he had served with, people who had known Luis and shared in his pain.

The service was somber, filled with the weight of unspoken grief. As the priest spoke about Luis's life, his service, and the impact he had made on those around him, Jack found himself slipping further into his own thoughts. The words washed over him, barely registering, as he stared at the coffin at the front of the church, draped in the American flag.

When it was time for the eulogies, Mike stood up to speak, his voice breaking as he talked about the good times they had shared, the bond they had formed during their years of service. Jack listened, feeling the guilt tighten its grip on his chest with every word. He should have been the one up there, should have been the one to say something, but he couldn't. He couldn't find the words, couldn't find the strength to speak about a man he felt he had failed.

After the service, they moved to the cemetery for the burial. The air was heavy with sorrow as the coffin was lowered into the ground, the finality of it settling over everyone like a shroud. Jack stood at the edge of the grave, staring down at the casket, his heart breaking under the weight of his grief.

When the ceremony ended, people began to drift away, offering their condolences to Luis's family before leaving. Jack stayed behind, unable to tear himself away from the grave. He felt Emma's hand on his arm, her silent support steadying him, but the darkness inside him felt too powerful, too consuming.

"I need a minute," Jack said quietly, not looking at her.

Emma hesitated, clearly reluctant to leave him alone, but she nodded. "I'll be in the car," she said, squeezing his arm before turning to go.

Jack waited until everyone else had left, until he was alone with Luis's grave. The wind picked up, rustling the leaves in the trees, and Jack felt a cold chill run down his spine. He knelt by the grave, his hands resting on the freshly turned earth, his head bowed.

"I'm sorry, Luis," he whispered, his voice thick with emotion. "I'm so damn sorry. I should have been there for you. I should have done more."

The wind howled around him, carrying his words away, and Jack felt a sob rise in his throat. He had thought he was getting better, thought he was finally finding some peace, but Luis's death had ripped open old wounds, leaving him raw and vulnerable.

"I don't know how to do this," Jack said, his voice breaking. "I don't know how to keep going when it feels like everything is falling apart."

Tears streamed down his face as he knelt there, the grief and guilt pouring out of him in a torrent. He had tried so hard to move forward, to make something good out of the pain, but now it all felt like a lie. Luis was gone, and nothing Jack did could change that. No amount of volunteering, no amount of therapy, could bring him back.

The sound of footsteps behind him made Jack turn, and he saw Mike standing there, his expression somber. He walked over and knelt beside Jack, placing a hand on his shoulder.

"It's not your fault, Jack," Mike said quietly, his voice filled with understanding. "None of us saw it coming. We all missed the signs. But that doesn't mean we didn't care or that we didn't try. Sometimes... sometimes, people make choices we can't control, no matter how much we wish we could."

Jack nodded, but the words offered little comfort. The guilt was a living thing, coiled tight in his chest, refusing to let go. "I just feel like I failed him," Jack said, his voice barely above a whisper. "Like I should have done more."

Mike squeezed his shoulder. "We all feel that way, Jack. We've all lost friends, brothers, sisters... it's part of this life we live. But carrying that guilt alone—it'll eat you alive. You know that better than anyone. We have to lean on each other. That's the only way we survive this."

Jack wiped at his eyes, trying to pull himself together. "I thought I was getting better, Mike. I really did. But now... now I don't know."

Mike looked at him, his gaze steady and unwavering. "You are getting better, Jack. But healing isn't a straight line. There are setbacks, bad days. Days like today, when it feels like the world is caving in on you. But that doesn't erase the progress you've made. It doesn't mean you're back at square one."

Jack took a deep breath, trying to absorb Mike's words. He knew Mike was right, but it was hard to see the progress when the pain was so fresh, so raw. He had spent months building himself back up, only to feel like he was crumbling all over again.

"What do we do now?" Jack asked, his voice thick with emotion. "How do we keep going after this?"

Mike was silent for a moment, his eyes fixed on the grave in front of them. "We remember Luis for the good man he was. We honor his memory by living our lives in a way that would make him proud. And we keep fighting—fighting for ourselves, for each other, and for all the people who didn't make it back."

Jack nodded slowly, the resolve in Mike's words seeping into him. He had to keep going. For Luis, for the others they had lost, for Emma and Lily, and for himself. Even when it felt impossible, even when the guilt threatened to pull him under, he had to keep fighting.

Together, Jack and Mike stood, the weight of the moment heavy on their shoulders. They exchanged a look, a silent understanding passing between them. They had both been through hell and back, and they would carry the scars for the rest of their lives. But they weren't alone. They had each other, and they had the strength that came from surviving, from enduring.

As they walked back to the car, Jack felt the first drops of rain start to fall, mingling with the tears that still clung to his face. The sky opened up, a cold, steady downpour, as if the heavens were mourning Luis's loss alongside them.

When they reached the car, Emma was waiting, her eyes filled with concern. Jack didn't say anything; he just reached for her, pulling her into a tight embrace. She held him close, her warmth grounding him, reminding him that there was still good in the world, still love, still hope.

They drove home in silence, the rain pattering against the windows, the grief hanging heavy in the air. Jack stared out at the passing landscape, his mind a storm of emotions. He knew the road ahead would be hard—harder than he had ever imagined—but he also knew he couldn't give up. He had come too far to let the darkness win now.

Over the next few days, the pain of Luis's death lingered like a shadow over Jack's life. The Outreach Center felt different, quieter, as if everyone there was carrying the same weight of loss. Jack threw himself into his work, trying to distract himself from the pain, but it was always there, just beneath the surface.

One afternoon, Greg approached Jack, his expression serious. "How are you holding up?" he asked, his voice low.

Jack shrugged, not sure how to answer. "I'm managing," he said, though it didn't feel like the truth.

Greg nodded, as if he understood. "I know this has been a tough week for you. For all of us. But I want you to know how much we appreciate what you're doing here. The veterans you've been helping—they're making real progress because of you. You're making a difference, Jack."

Jack looked at Greg, feeling a flicker of something—gratitude, maybe, or hope. "Thanks, Greg. I'm just trying to do what I can."

"You're doing more than that," Greg said. "And I think you know that. I don't want you to lose sight of how far you've come, even in the face of this tragedy. You've been a rock for a lot of people here. Don't forget that."

Jack nodded, trying to let Greg's words sink in. It was hard, especially with the fresh grief still gnawing at him, but he knew Greg was right. He couldn't let Luis's death undo everything he had worked for. He had to keep moving forward, even when it felt like the world was crumbling around him.

Later that night, as Jack sat in the living room with Emma, he finally found the words he had been searching for all day.

"I've been thinking a lot about what Mike said," Jack began, his voice quiet. "About how we have to honor the people we've lost by living in a way that would make them proud."

Emma looked up from the book she was reading, her eyes soft with understanding. "He's right, you know. You've been doing that, Jack. You've been honoring Luis and all the others by helping people, by being there for them when they need it most."

Jack nodded, but there was still a heaviness in his chest. "I know, but it's hard not to feel like I failed him. Like there was something I could have done to stop this from happening."

Emma reached out, taking his hand in hers. "You did everything you could, Jack. You've been fighting your own battles, and you've come so far. Luis made his own choices, and as much as you want to, you can't take that burden on yourself. What you can do is keep going, keep helping others, and keep living your life in a way that would make Luis proud."

Jack squeezed her hand, finding comfort in her words. "I'm trying, Em. I really am. It's just... hard."

"I know it is," she said, her voice gentle. "But you're not alone in this. I'm here, and so is everyone at the Outreach Center, everyone at the VFW. We're all in this together."

Jack leaned back on the couch, his mind turning over the events of the past few days. The pain of losing Luis would never fully go away, he knew that. But he also knew that he couldn't let it consume him. He had to find a way to live with it, to carry the memory of his friend with him without letting it drag him down.

As he sat there, surrounded by the warmth of his home and the love of his family, Jack decided. He would keep fighting, not just for himself, but for Luis and for everyone else who had been lost to the darkness. He would honor their memories by living his life with purpose, by helping others, and by refusing to give up, no matter how hard things got.

The road ahead was still uncertain, still filled with challenges, but Jack knew now that he wasn't walking it alone. He had Emma, he had Lily, and he had the community of veterans who understood his pain, who shared in it, and who were fighting their own battles every day.

And with them by his side, Jack knew he could face whatever came next. He would keep going, keep living, and keep fighting—for himself, for his family, and for all the people he had loved and lost along the way.

The next morning, Jack woke up early, feeling a renewed sense of determination. He knew that the battle with his inner demons was far from over, but he also knew that he had the strength to keep going. He got dressed and headed to the Outreach Center, ready to face the day, ready to help others, and ready to continue the work that gave his life meaning.

As he walked through the doors of the center, Jack felt a sense of purpose settle over him. He wasn't just surviving anymore; he was living. And that, he realized, was the greatest victory of all.

The battle wasn't over, but Jack knew he was winning. One day at a time, one step at a time, he was finding his way back to himself. And as long as he kept moving forward, he knew he would eventually find peace.

CHAPTER 9: CONFRONTING THE PAST

As the weeks went by, Jack threw himself into his work at the Veterans Outreach Center, channeling his pain and guilt into helping others. The new leadership role Greg had offered him provided a sense of purpose, something to hold on to when the darkness threatened to pull him under. But no matter how much progress he made; Jack knew that there was one thing he still hadn't faced—one memory that haunted him more than any other.

The mission. The village. The boy.

No amount of work, no number of therapy sessions, could erase what had happened that day. The faces of the villagers who had died under his command—the boy who had bled out in his arms—were etched into his mind, haunting his dreams, lurking in the shadows of his thoughts. Jack had tried to bury the memory, to drown it out with work and service, but it was always there, a constant reminder of his deepest shame.

One afternoon, after another difficult session with Dr. Barnes, Jack finally admitted what had been eating away at him.

"I can't stop thinking about the mission," Jack said, his voice strained. "The one where everything went wrong. I see their faces every time I close my eyes. The boy… he was so young, and I couldn't save him."

Dr. Barnes nodded, her expression gentle and understanding. "You've mentioned this mission before, Jack, but we've never really delved into it. It's clear that this is a central part of your pain. Maybe it's time we confront it directly."

Jack swallowed hard, the thought of reliving that day making his stomach turn. "I don't know if I can," he admitted. "I don't know if I'm strong enough."

"You are strong enough," Dr. Barnes said firmly. "You've been carrying this burden for too long, Jack. It's time to face it, to really look at it, and to start the process of healing from it. We can take it slow, but I think it's important for you to confront this part of your past."

Jack sat in silence for a long time, his mind churning. He had been running from that day for so long, afraid to look too closely, afraid of what he might find if he did. But he also knew that Dr. Barnes was right. He couldn't move forward until he confronted the memory that had been haunting him for so many years.

"How do I even begin?" Jack asked, his voice barely above a whisper.

"We start by talking about it," Dr. Barnes said gently. "You don't have to relive every detail right now, but I want you to tell me what happened in your own words. Let's take it one step at a time."

Jack nodded, taking a deep breath. He closed his eyes, trying to steady himself, and then he began to speak.

"We were supposed to be taking out an insurgent stronghold," Jack began, his voice shaking slightly. "The intel was solid—or so we thought. It was supposed to be a straightforward mission. In and out. But... when we got there, everything went to hell."

He could still remember the heat of the

desert sun, the dust swirling in the air as they approached the village. The tension in the air had been palpable, the sense that something wasn't right gnawing at his gut. But they had their orders, and Jack had led his men into the village, weapons ready, hearts pounding.

"We breached the compound, expecting to find enemy fighters," Jack continued, his voice growing more strained. "But instead, we found civilians. Women, children, old men… It was a massacre. Shots were fired before we realized what was happening. By the time I managed to call off the attack, it was too late."

He could still see the bodies on the ground, the blood soaking into the dirt. The cries of the wounded, the shock and fear on the faces of the survivors, haunted him every day. But it was the boy—no older than Lily—who had broken him.

"There was this boy," Jack said, his voice cracking. "He was lying on the ground, bleeding out. I tried to save him, but… I couldn't. He died in my arms. I can still see his face, feel his blood on my hands. And I knew… I knew that I was responsible for it all."

Tears streamed down Jack's face as he spoke, the memory too vivid, too real. He had buried it for so long, but now that it was out in the open, the pain was overwhelming.

Dr. Barnes waited for a moment, letting Jack catch his breath before she spoke. "Jack, what you experienced that day was a profound moral injury. You were put in an impossible situation, one where the lines between right and wrong became blurred. But you were also following orders, trying to protect your men, trying to complete the mission as you were trained to do."

"I know that logically," Jack said, wiping his eyes. "But it doesn't make it any easier to live with. I made the call. I gave the orders. And because of that, people died."

"You were in a war zone," Dr. Barnes said gently. "Mistakes happen. Tragedies happen. But it's important to remember that you didn't set out to harm anyone. You were doing your job in an incredibly complex and dangerous situation. What happened was terrible, but it doesn't define you as a person."

Jack nodded, though the guilt still weighed heavily on his chest. "I just keep thinking... what if I had done something differently? What if I had questioned the intel? What if I had been more cautious?"

Dr. Barnes leaned forward slightly, her gaze intense but compassionate. "Those 'what ifs' can tear you apart, Jack. But they're not fair to you. You made the best decisions you could with the information you had at the time. You can't go back and change the past, but you can work on accepting it, on finding a way to forgive yourself."

Jack looked down at his hands, the memory of the boy's blood still vivid in his mind. "How do I do that?" he asked, his voice small. "How do I forgive myself for something like that?"

"It's not something that happens overnight," Dr. Barnes said. "It's a process, one that takes time and a lot of self-compassion. But one way to start is by finding a way to honor the lives that were lost. You've already started doing that through your work at the Outreach Center, but perhaps there's more you can do. Maybe it's time to revisit that place, to confront it head-on."

Jack felt a chill run down his spine at the thought of returning to the village. He hadn't been back since that day, hadn't even allowed himself to think about it as a real place, just a nightmare that existed only in his mind. But maybe Dr. Barnes was right. Maybe facing it in person, standing on that ground again, could help him start to heal.

"Do you think that could help?" Jack asked, his voice trembling.

"I think it could be a powerful step toward healing," Dr. Barnes said. "It won't be easy, but sometimes facing the source of our pain can help us begin to let it go. And you don't have to do it alone. You could take someone with you—Mike, perhaps, or Emma—someone who can support you through it."

Jack sat with the idea for a moment,

feeling the fear gnawing at him, but also a strange sense of resolve. It was terrifying, the thought of returning to that place, of facing the ghosts that haunted him. But he also knew that he couldn't keep running forever. If he was ever going to find peace, he had to confront the past head-on.

"I'll think about it," Jack said finally, his voice quiet but determined.

Dr. Barnes smiled, a look of approval in her eyes. "That's all I ask, Jack. You've come so far, and I believe you have the strength to take this next step when you're ready."

The rest of the session passed in a blur, but the idea of returning to the village stayed with Jack long after he left Dr. Barnes's office. That night, as he lay in bed beside Emma, he couldn't stop thinking about it—about what it would mean to go back, to see the place where his life had changed forever.

The next morning, over breakfast, Jack decided to broach the subject with Emma.

"Dr. Barnes suggested something yesterday," Jack began, his voice tentative. "Something that... scares the hell out of me, but might help me move forward."

Emma looked up from her coffee, her expression concerned. "What is it?"

"She thinks I should go back to the village," Jack said, the words heavy in his mouth. "The one where the mission went wrong. She thinks it could help me start to heal, to confront what happened there."

Emma's eyes widened, a mixture of shock and worry crossing her face. "Jack... that's a big step. Are you sure you're ready for something like that?"

Jack sighed, running a hand through his hair. "I don't know if I'm ready, but I think I need to do it. I can't keep running from this, Emma. I can't keep letting it control my life."

Emma reached across the table, taking his hand in hers. "If you think this will help, then I support you. But you don't have to do it alone. If you want me to come with you, I will."

Jack squeezed her hand, grateful for her unwavering support. "Thank you, Em. I don't know if I could do this without you."

A few weeks later, after planning and preparing himself as much as he could for what lay ahead, Jack found himself standing at the edge of a dusty road in a remote part of the Middle East, the same place where his life had changed forever. The village was smaller than he remembered, its buildings weathered and worn, as if the passage of time had taken its toll on the physical world as much as it had on his soul. The air was thick with the scent of dust and dry earth, the heat of the sun bearing down on him as he took in the familiar yet distant scene.

Emma stood beside him, her hand wrapped firmly around his, offering silent support. She had insisted on coming with him, and though Jack had initially hesitated, he was grateful for her presence now. Mike had wanted to come too, but Jack knew this was something he needed to face with Emma, the person who had been with him through the worst of it, who had seen him at his lowest and still loved him.

Jack took a deep breath, trying to steady himself as they walked down the road leading into the heart of the village. His heart pounded in his chest, each step feeling like a lead weight as he approached the place where his memories had been born. Every part of him wanted to turn back, to run away from the pain and guilt that awaited him, but he knew that this was the only way forward. He couldn't keep hiding from his past.

As they entered the village, the first thing Jack noticed was the silence. It was eerie, almost surreal, the kind of quiet that felt unnatural, as if the village itself were holding its breath, waiting for something to happen. The buildings were as he remembered them—simple, made of mud bricks and stone, with small windows and wooden doors. Some of the houses were abandoned, their doors hanging open, their interiors dark and empty. Others showed signs of life, but there were no people in sight, as if the village had retreated inward, away from the world.

They walked past the spot where the initial firefight had broken out, where the chaos had started. Jack could still see it in his mind—the shouts of his men, the crack of gunfire, the confusion as they realized too late that they had made a terrible mistake. He stopped for a moment, the memories flooding back with such intensity that he had to close his eyes, his breath catching in his throat.

Emma squeezed his hand, grounding him in the present. "Jack, it's okay. Take your time."

Jack nodded, forcing himself to open his eyes, to confront the place where everything had gone wrong. "This is where it started," he said quietly. "This is where we first realized… where I first realized what we had done."

They continued walking until they reached the center of the village, where a small, makeshift market had been set up. A few people milled about, their expressions wary as they noticed Jack and Emma. Jack could feel their eyes on him, could feel the weight of their judgment, whether it was real or imagined. These were the people who had survived, who had witnessed the devastation he had caused. He felt like an intruder, an unwelcome reminder of a past they had tried to move beyond.

"Do you want to talk to anyone?" Emma asked gently, her voice filled with concern.

"I don't know," Jack admitted, his voice strained. "I don't even know what I would say."

As they stood there, an older man approached them, his face lined with age and weariness. He wore a simple tunic and headscarf, his eyes dark and unreadable as he looked at Jack. For a moment, Jack was sure the man recognized him, but then he realized that wasn't possible. Too much time had passed. But the man's gaze was piercing, as if he could see the weight Jack carried, the burden of guilt that had brought him back to this place.

"Do you need help?" the man asked in broken English, his voice rough but not unkind.

Jack hesitated, searching for the right words. "I... I was here before," he said slowly, the words feeling heavy on his tongue. "A long time ago. I'm... I'm sorry for what happened."

The man studied him for a long moment, his expression unreadable. Jack braced himself for anger, for hostility, but instead, the man simply nodded. "We remember," he said. "Many things happened here. Many people lost. But we also remember those who try to make amends."

Jack felt a lump rise in his throat, the man's words cutting through him like a knife. "I don't know if I can ever make up for what happened," he said, his voice trembling. "But I'm trying. I'm trying to live differently, to do something good with the life I still have."

The man's expression softened, and he reached out to place a hand on Jack's shoulder. "You are here," he said simply. "That means something. It means you carry the memory, and you do not forget. That is enough."

Jack felt tears sting his eyes, and he blinked them back, overwhelmed by the man's unexpected kindness. He had come here expecting condemnation, expecting to be rejected, but instead, he had found a small measure of understanding, of acceptance.

"Thank you," Jack said, his voice thick with emotion. "Thank you for saying that."

The man nodded again, then turned and walked away, leaving Jack and Emma standing alone in the center of the village. Jack watched him go, the man's words echoing in his mind. You carry the memory, and you do not forget. That is enough.

"Are you okay?" Emma asked, her voice soft as she looked up at him, her eyes filled with concern.

Jack took a deep breath, letting the tension in his chest slowly ease. "Yeah," he said, surprising himself with the realization that he meant it. "I think I am."

They spent the next few hours walking through the village, retracing the steps of that fateful day. Jack didn't shy away from the places that hurt the most, the places where the memories were sharpest. He let himself feel the pain, the guilt, the sorrow, but he also let himself accept that what was done couldn't be undone. It was a part of him, a scar he would carry for the rest of his life, but it didn't have to define him.

As they prepared to leave, Jack took one last look at the village. The sun was beginning to set, casting long shadows over the ground, the light turning golden as it filtered through the dust in the air. There was a strange sense of peace here, a quiet acceptance that felt like a balm to Jack's wounded soul. He knew he would never forget what had happened in this place, but for the first time, he felt like he could live with it.

"Thank you for coming with me," Jack said as they walked back to their car, his voice quiet.

Emma smiled, her hand still holding his. "I wouldn't have let you do this alone. I'm proud of you, Jack. This was a huge step."

Jack nodded, feeling a sense of closure that he hadn't expected. "It was. And I think... I think I'm ready to keep moving forward now."

They drove back to the city in comfortable silence, the weight that had been pressing on Jack's chest slowly lifting. He knew there would still be hard days, still moments when the memories would overwhelm him, but he also knew that he had faced his past head-on, that he had taken the first step toward true healing.

When they returned home, Jack felt a

sense of lightness, a sense of possibility that he hadn't felt in years. He had come to terms with what had happened, had accepted that the past couldn't be changed, but the future was still his to shape.

That night, as they lay in bed, Emma turned to him, her expression soft in the dim light.

"What now?" she asked, her voice barely above a whisper.

Jack thought about it for a moment, the answer coming to him as naturally as breathing. "Now, we live. We keep moving forward, one day at a time. And we don't forget, but we don't let it hold us back either."

Emma smiled, her eyes shining with love. "I like that plan."

Jack pulled her close, feeling the steady

rhythm of her heartbeat against his chest. He had faced the darkest parts of himself, had confronted the pain and guilt that had been eating away at him for so long. And now, he was ready to move forward, ready to live the life that had been given back to him.

As he closed his eyes, he felt a sense of peace settle over him, a peace that came from knowing that while the past would always be a part of him, it didn't have to define him. The future was his to shape, and he was ready to face it with open arms, surrounded by the love and support of those who mattered most.

The road ahead would still have its challenges, but Jack knew that he wasn't walking it alone. He had Emma, he had Lily, and he had the strength that came from surviving, from enduring, and from choosing to keep going, no matter how hard it got.

And for the first time in a long while, Jack truly believed that he was going to be okay. He had faced the past, and now, he was ready to embrace the future.

CHAPTER 10: EMBRACING THE FUTURE

The days following Jack's return from the village were marked by a profound change in him. The memories of that day still lingered, but they no longer had the same power to paralyze him with guilt. Instead, they became a part of his story—something he had survived, something that had shaped him, but not something that defined his entire existence. Jack had faced the darkness, and while it would always be with him, he had learned to carry it in a way that allowed him to move forward.

Emma noticed the change too. Jack was more present, more engaged with their life together. He smiled more, laughed more, and the weight that had been pressing down on him for so long seemed to have lifted. He was still the man who had been through hell, but now there was a lightness in him, a sense of peace that she hadn't seen in years.

One evening, as they sat together on the porch, watching the sun set over the horizon, Emma turned to Jack, a thoughtful expression on her face.

"You seem… different," she said, her voice soft. "Happier. More at peace."

Jack nodded, a small smile tugging at the corners of his mouth. "I think I am," he said. "Going back to the village… it was hard, but it helped me make peace with what happened. I'm not running from it anymore. I've accepted that it's a part of me, but it doesn't have to control me."

Emma reached out, taking his hand in hers. "I'm so proud of you, Jack. You've come so far. We've come so far."

Jack squeezed her hand, feeling a deep sense of gratitude for everything they had been through together. "I couldn't have done it without you, Em. You've been my rock through all of this."

Emma smiled, leaning into him, resting her head on his shoulder. "We've been each other's rock. And I'm just so glad to have you back—to really have you back."

Jack kissed the top of her head, feeling a swell of love for the woman who had stood by him through everything, who had never given up on him, even when he had almost given up on himself.

"We're in this together," Jack said, his voice filled with emotion. "And I'm not going anywhere. Not now, not ever."

The days turned into weeks, and Jack continued to embrace the future he was building. His work at the Veterans

Outreach Center grew even more meaningful as he stepped into his new leadership role. He found himself mentoring other veterans, guiding them through the job placement process, and helping them navigate the challenges of transitioning back into civilian life. Each success, each veteran who found a job, who started to rebuild their life, felt like a victory for Jack too—a way of making amends for the past, of giving back in a way that honored the lives of those he had lost.

One day, Greg approached Jack with an idea that had been brewing for some time.

"Jack, you've been doing incredible work here," Greg said, clapping him on the back. "I was thinking… how would you feel about starting a new program? Something specifically focused on helping veterans deal with PTSD and moral injury—something that combines therapy, peer support, and job training."

Jack felt a surge of excitement at the idea. It was exactly the kind of work that had helped him so much, and he knew it could make a huge difference in the lives of others who were struggling.

"I think that's a great idea," Jack said, his mind already racing with possibilities. "There are so many vets out there who need this kind of support—people who feel like they're alone, like there's no way out. If we can reach them, if we can give them hope, that would be… that would be everything."

Greg smiled, clearly pleased with Jack's enthusiasm. "I knew you'd be the right person for this, Jack. Let's start putting together a plan, and we'll take it from there."

Over the next few weeks, Jack worked closely with Greg and other team members at the center to develop the new program. They reached out to local therapists, including Dr. Barnes, who was more than willing to lend her expertise. They also connected with other veterans' organizations and community resources to create a comprehensive support network for those who needed it most.

The program, which they named Operation Resilience, launched with a small group of veterans who were struggling with PTSD and moral injury. Jack led the sessions, drawing on his own experiences to guide the discussions, and he quickly saw the impact it was having. The veterans who joined the program began to open up, sharing their stories, their pain, and their hopes for the future. And as they did, Jack could see the healing start to take place—not just for them, but for himself as well.

One evening, after a particularly powerful session, Jack stayed behind at the center, tidying up the room where they held the meetings. As he worked, he felt a deep sense of fulfillment, something he hadn't felt in a long time. He knew he was doing exactly what he was meant to do—helping others find their way out of the darkness, just as he had found his.

As Jack was about to leave, he noticed one of the veterans from the session, a young man named Chris, standing by the door, hesitating as if he wanted to say something but wasn't sure how to start.

"Hey, Chris," Jack said, walking over to him. "Everything okay?"

Chris nodded, though he seemed nervous. "Yeah, I just... I wanted to say thank you, Jack. For this program, for everything you've been doing. I've been struggling for so long, and I never thought I'd find a way out. But... this is helping. You're helping. And I just wanted you to know that."

Jack felt a lump rise in his throat, the young man's words hitting him harder than he expected. "You're doing the hard work, Chris. I'm just here to help guide the way. But I'm glad it's making a difference for you."

Chris looked down at the floor, his voice quiet. "You've been through a lot too, haven't you? It helps, knowing that you get it, that you understand what it's like. That means a lot."

Jack nodded, his heart heavy with the weight of their shared experiences. "I do understand, Chris. And that's why I'm here—because I want to make sure that no one else has to go through this alone. We're in this together, all of us."

Chris smiled, a small but genuine smile, and Jack felt a deep sense of connection with the young man. They were both survivors, both fighting their own battles, but they were also part of something bigger—a community that understood, that supported, that cared.

As Chris left, Jack stood alone in the empty room, his mind filled with thoughts of the journey that had brought him here. He had come so far, had faced so many demons, but he had also found a way to live with the past, to find meaning in the present, and to build a future he could be proud of.

When Jack finally returned home that night, he found Emma waiting for him on the porch, a cup of tea in her hands. She looked up as he approached, her face lighting up with a smile.

"How was the session?" she asked, her voice warm and inviting.

Jack sat down beside her, feeling the tension of the day melt away in her presence. "It was good. Better than good, actually. I think we're really making a difference, Em. It feels… right."

Emma reached over, taking his hand in hers. "I'm so happy for you, Jack. You've worked so hard to get to this place, and you deserve to feel proud of what you've accomplished."

Jack squeezed her hand, his heart full of gratitude. "I couldn't have done it without you," he said softly. "You've been my anchor through all of this."

Emma smiled, her eyes filled with love. "And you've been mine."

As they sat together, watching the stars

twinkle in the night sky, Jack felt a deep sense of contentment, a peace that had once seemed so far out of reach. He had faced his past, had made peace with it, and had found a way to live with the scars it had left behind. And now, he was building a future—one filled with love, with purpose, and with hope.

The road ahead would still have its challenges, but Jack knew that he had the strength to face them. He had come through the fire, had faced the darkest parts of himself, and had emerged on the other side, stronger and more determined than ever. He was ready to embrace the future, to live his life fully, and to help others do the same.

As the night deepened, Jack and Emma sat together, their hands intertwined, their hearts full. The journey they had taken together had been long and difficult, but it had also brought them closer, had shown them the power of love, of resilience, of never giving up.

And as they looked out into the vast expanse of the night sky, they knew that whatever the future held, they would face it together—stronger, wiser, and more connected than ever before.

Jack had found his way home, and now, he was ready to live.

THE

END

Made in the USA
Columbia, SC
09 January 2025

2a43723f-3f30-4634-8fc6-0f66db01c691R02